LOVE
Machine

KENDALL RYAN

About the Book

After a rather uncomfortable ladies' night involving a cucumber-wielding instructor with judgy eyes, I'm forced to admit my weaknesses. Rather than point blame at my lack of a sex life, I'm ready to roll up my sleeves and get to work.

As a junior executive who's clawed her way up the corporate ladder, failure is not in my vocabulary. Confident and bold in other areas of my life, I have to admit it's time to up my bedroom game.

Asking my best friend, Slate Cruz, is really the only option. Slate is like a walking billboard for sex. The man gets more ass than a toilet seat. There's no way I'll want more from this playboy than a little inspiration to revive my inner sex kitten.

Except, what happens if I do?

CHAPTER
One

Keaton

GRIN AND BEAR IT.

It's a familiar phrase to those of us who spend most of our lives people-pleasing. But I, Keaton Henley, software saleswoman and best friend extraordinaire, don't just grin and bear it at my favorite person's bachelorette party. I grin and *wear* it.

"This is so much fun!" I say to the woman of the hour, Karina. We've been besties since our college days, back when the parties were in dimly lit fraternity houses and the drinks were almost exclusively mixed with cheap vodka.

I squeeze her arm, overwhelmed with a moment of nostalgia. She almost spills her mimosa on both of us.

"You're not fooling anyone," Karina whispers drunkenly to me, her brown eyes boring deep holes into my fraudulent enthusiasm.

"What? Are you kidding?" I lie, finger guns poised. "This is so. Much. Fun." *Pow, pow, pow.*

The women around us at the bachelorette party sit in an amiable circle in the beautiful living room, lounging on plush couches and pillows, chattering about their latest sexual encounters. Ariana, Karina's younger sister, roommate, and maid of honor, speaks in the loudest drunken whisper, explaining in heightened detail the unexpected pleasures of anal sex.

Everyone is much drunker than me, but that's pretty normal in our friend group. At this time of day, I'm usually on my third cup of coffee, not my third cocktail. Okay, that's an exaggeration, but still.

Karina raises her eyebrows at my smoking fingers. "You always use finger guns when you're lying, Keaton."

I shoot her again, just for fun. She rolls her eyes, so I grab her hand and plant a quick kiss on it.

"The estrogen level in this room is just higher than what I'm used to," I remind her.

I work with a software sales team that is highly male-dominated. Reconnecting with our female college friends and meeting some of Karina's female co-workers for the first time has been a change of speed that takes some getting used to. Usually, my daily conversations consist of maximizing sales, expanding our demographic, and developing new marketing techniques. Today, we're all listening to Ariana talk about maximizing pleasure, expanding her list of partners, and developing new sex techniques.

"It's all about trust," Ariana says in that adorably frustrating been-there-done-that voice. She's answered by collective head nods, led by my other friend Gabby, who raises her glass with triumph.

"To anal!" Gabby cries, winking at both Karina and me.

Gabby is probably the most sexually adventurous creature I've ever known; she's had notches etched on her bedpost since she was fifteen. All curves and confidence, she got every kind of ass imaginable back when Karina and I were too busy getting every kind of blown off.

Karina finishes her drink in one big gulp and takes my hand. "Come on. I need something stronger."

She yanks me up, and we scuttle away from the couches of the trendy living room into the even trendier kitchenette. Karina knows just where her sister's whiskey stash is: tucked behind the olive oil on the top shelf. As she unscrews the cap and pours the contents into two coffee mugs, we listen to

Ariana begin another story about an entirely different adventure of the sexual nature.

"Why does your sister always have the best sex
stories? Isn't she like, five years younger than us?" I
ask mournfully.

Karina laughs, sipping on her whiskey with a
smile. "She's a tornado. Wait till you hear what she
has planned for the rest of the party."

"More drinking, I hope."

"Oh yes. You'll definitely need to drink more for
what's coming."

That doesn't sound promising.

As if on cue, there's a knock at the door. My ears
perk up and I lean around the kitchen island to get a
look down the front hall.

Gabby races to answer the door. "Coming!" she
calls, throwing open the door. Turning back to look
over her shoulder at the rest of the ladies, she smirks
and says, "Well, we all will be soon."

A woman stands there dressed in a flouncy sun-
dress with a matching picnic basket and bright red
lipstick. "Hello, there," she says with a smile, holding
out her hand.

Gabby takes in her hand and then immediately
stares at the unassuming woman's boobs. "Whoa.
Holy knockers," she purrs.

Karina groans into her mug, and I laugh. Shameless, that woman.

Ariana is quick to the door, pulling the woman into the apartment she shares with her sister like she's about to introduce us to the living embodiment of the cure for cancer. "Everyone, meet Claire! Claire is our best friend today, because she's going to change our lives."

"I don't know about that." Claire laughs. She looks to be in her mid-twenties.

Oh, to be five years younger and pull off that kind of cleavage again.

She begins to unpack the contents of her picnic basket on the coffee table—lotions, towels, cucumbers. Our friends lean in, intrigued.

"Oh yes, spa time!" I cheer, setting down my whiskey with a clink on the countertop, and then skip over to embrace my bliss.

"Somehow I don't think that's what—" Karina calls after me, but it's too late.

I snatch up one of the cucumbers, looking at Claire with a grin. "Hi. I prefer these in my stomach rather than on my eyes," I explain, pretty sure the whiskey has stolen my filter.

Claire's red lips curl into a smile as my own wrap around the vegetable, preparing for a bite. "Actually," she says, "those are for the oral-sex presentation."

Crunch. I feel my cheeks flame up as my friends all explode into laugher.

"Oh, all right," I mumble through a mouthful of cucumber. "Get it out of your systems, ladies."

I look to Karina in the kitchen with a desperate plea for help.

She merely raises her mug to me. "Let's get started."

♥

Standing in the front hall of Ariana and Karina's apartment, I hug Karina good-bye, swaying back and forth in my tipsiness. The other women are changing into their sexy bar outfits, waltzing around in various levels of undress.

They're ready to hit the town after pregaming with Claire and her cucumbers. Me? I'm ready for bed.

I whisper drunkenly in Karina's ear. "I love you so much—so, so much. Please just kill me now while you're at the prime of your happiness and I'm at the lowest of lows."

"It wasn't that bad," she says, patting my back.

It was *that* bad. I slobbered all over my cucumber, making a complete mess of myself and becoming tonight's source of entertainment for all our friends. Their stomach muscles are probably aching with how hard they laughed at me.

"I wish you could stay." She sighs. "I never get to see you anymore. And I'm getting married, which means I probably will be no more fun and I'll see you even less."

"Nonsense," I say, planting a kiss on her cheek. I've learned my lesson about staying out late with these ladies. Don't—unless you have time to nurse a wicked hangover in the morning.

"Okay." She pouts, reaching up to straighten my glasses, slightly askew from our bear hug. "See you soon?"

"I promise, missy." I smile.

"Promissy," she slurs back.

"Gabby," I call over Karina's shoulder, and Gabby pokes her head out of the bathroom, wearing only her underthings and wielding a curling iron. "Please remember to watch out for our girl tonight? And don't disappear with some rando?"

She smiles and flips me off. It's just like college again.

"Love you all!" I declare to the masses, and am met with a chorus of love from my favorite people. I close the door behind me and release a deep sigh.

A sense of restlessness courses through me as I stand on the street, waiting for my Uber to arrive. The night air is jolting, seeming to magnify my every emotion.

God, that was humiliating. I curse at myself for being so sexually behind everyone else. I thought my blow jobs were average; I didn't think I was *that* bad. Claire's annoying little twenty-something smirk had me sweating balls.

I remember how I dropped the cucumber on the floor, my hands slick with nerves and my own spit.

Claire had smiled encouragingly and said, in front of everyone, "Don't worry, Keaton. I doubt you'll make anyone's dick fall off . . . Well, not unless you bite down, that is."

Bitch.

My Uber pulls up. I climb inside the dim interior and slam the door with more force than necessary, worried that I'm going to turn into a scary, angry, sexless woman.

A small voice in my head reminds me that I'm good at so many things. I went to a goddamn Ivy League school, for crying out loud. But perfect attendance and an honor roll certificate don't mean that I know how to roll my tongue around a cock, and that's what I'm currently fixated on.

I pull out my phone. Lists always help me sort through my thoughts. I recall Ariana's stories and tap my fingers against the screen rapidly.

<u>Keaton's To-Do List for Sex</u>
Number 1: Blow jobs.
Number 2: Dirty talk.
Number 3: New positions.
Number 4: Anal.
Num—

My typing is interrupted by a nagging thought. *Keaton*, it pokes, *you're single. Are you going to go out every night and hook up with randos, hoping they'll be cool with you experimenting sexually on them?*

That sounds exhausting. I groan, tossing my phone in my bag. My head lands with a thud against the uncomfortable headrest.

"You okay?" the driver asks.

"You bet," I say, finger guns popping.

Buzz. Someone is texting me.

I dig around my bag for my phone. SLATE CRUZ, it reads.

You guys done with the bachelorette thing? I need my wing-woman.

I respond with lazy thumbs.

> I'm done, but I'm in no state
> to be anyone's wing-woman.

The Uber pulls up to my apartment building. I thank the driver and hobble to the elevator, fumbling for my keys. I need some ibuprofen and a blanket to bury myself in forever.

Drunk? Or tired?

> Both. Long day.

I can hear the familiar sound of Penny's aggravated meowing before I even open the door.

She glares up at me with her big green eyes, flashing all her teeth at me. *Feed me.*

"I know, Pen," I mutter. "Way past dinnertime."

I shed my coat, purse, and shoes before shuffling to the kitchen to dig out some food for the little monster. Penny follows close on my heels, pissed that she has to depend on a human for her sustenance. Which I totally get. I depend only on myself, which is just the way I like things.

"Here you go. Go crazy," I say, sneaking a quick

stroke across her back as she dives into her meal. She rarely lets me pet her now that she's grown, the little grump. I take what I can get when she chooses to dole out her affection.

I shuffle into my room to put on lazy clothes. I'm in the middle of piling my hair into a messy bun on top of my head when my phone buzzes again.

I'll pay for your ride here. Come on. I'm desperate. Look at me.

A picture message pops up of a coffee table covered in horrible snack foods: a half-eaten pizza, an opened energy drink, and some kind of nachos with . . . *chocolate* dribbled on top?

Buzz.

I'm spiraling in boredom.

I can't suppress a snort. My fingers fly across the keypad.

You don't need me by your side to get laid. Besides, I'm home now. I've taken off my bra. I'm in for the night. These are unchangeable truths.

I reopen the picture message. Yeah, that's definitely chocolate on his nachos.

I don't understand how this man lives. I met Slate during my freshman year of college through mutual friends, and now it seems like we've known each other forever. At first, I was floored by how ridiculously attractive he was. Tall, muscular, sharp brown eyes, soft brown hair, defined jaw, full lips, and a smile that could melt every heart in the room.

We became fast friends in no time. I was drawn to his fearlessness, his charisma, his sense of humor. Slate was totally willing to shoot the shit with me, unfazed by my "bossiness." It left an impression on me that developed into one of the most comfortable friendships I've ever had with a guy.

Buzz.

Fine. Tell me about the party. Were there strippers?

You would ask that.

What? Let me live vicariously through you.

Slate, you get plenty of ass.

> Let's not pretend my life
> is any wilder than it
> actually is.

He ignores this comment.

What's a bachelorette party without
strippers?

I sigh. Am I really going to tell him what the
main event of this party was?
Why not? The buzz of three mimosas and a whiskey still has me warm and fuzzy.

> Karina's sister booked a blow-
> job class. I sucked. Literally.

There's a slight delay before his next response.

I'm sure you were great.

> No, seriously. I bit the cucumber.

Oh my God, you didn't?

> I did.

That's like the only rule, Keat. No
teeth.

> That's why I suck. I suck at
> sucking. And I don't know how
> to get better.

The typing bubble starts, and then stops. Starts
again. Stops.

I frown at my phone. What's his deal? Finally, he
figures out what he wants to say.

Are you actually upset about this?

I roll my eyes. What a guy thing to say.

> Why wouldn't I be? I'm coming
> to terms with the fact that
> I'm not a sexually talented
> person. It's not exactly
> Christmas morning for me.

Oh, come on, you have to have skills.
Besides, you're gorgeous. You probably
just need a little practice.

I blink past the compliment. Slate has a habit of saying really wonderful things way too casually. I've always told him he's going to lead some poor girl on by being so nice all the time.

> What I need is boot camp.

Booty camp?

And then he ruins it. *Classic.*

Penny waddles into my room, her tummy full and round. She hops up on the bed and finds her favorite spot, curled up exactly in the center of the mattress. I've tried to fight her on this, but to no avail. I concede, wrapping my body around her warmth.

> I'm not joking, Slate. I feel
> really shitty about this.

The thought that sneaks up on me next comes out of nowhere. Before Sober Keaton can ruin it, Drunk Keaton takes the wheel for a gentle spin past the point of no return.

> Can I ask you something?

Sure.

My fingers are damn little traitors, typing away against my better judgment. I'm already plummeting down this rabbit shit-hole. Might as well make a splash?

> How about you stop making jokes and help me become a better lover?

Dead air. No typing bubble, no quippy response, nothing to break this tension I've created.

What have I done?

I toss the phone aside on my duvet and groan. Penny scoots away from me, displeased by my squirming. I've apparently interrupted something important, and she's less than thrilled.

Buzz.

Oh shit. I scramble for my phone, nearly elbowing the orange puffball dominating most of the bed.

> You want me to teach you how to fuck?

Well, that settles it.

> Forget it. I knew you'd make
> it a joke.

As soon as the message is delivered, my phone rings. He's calling me. Time for some damage control. I pick up.

"Hey, Slate, look—"

"I'm not making a joke." His voice sounds tight. Almost rigid. Which is so not Slate.

I can imagine him sitting on the edge of his couch with that look he gets on his face when he's really focused. Admittedly, it's not a bad look—his brow furrowed, gaze focused, thumb pressing against his bottom lip. It's kind of sexy, to be honest.

I let out a nervous little laugh. "I mean, I'm drunk. I don't know what I'm saying. I know you're probably not interested, anyway. Hell, you get more ass than a toilet seat at Taco Bell, and I'm not about to be sloppy seconds to your weekend plans. No offense—"

"Whoa, Keaton," he says. "I don't have any weekend plans."

"What does that mean?" I ask, my heart now galloping. Is this happening? Am I on the brink of making one of my best friendships totally, irrevocably weird?

"It means I could, well, take a break."

"Wow, so honorable," I say with a sneer.

"Come on, Keat, don't be like that." He sighs. I can imagine him running a hand through his hair, brushing it over the back of his neck.

"Sorry," I mumble. "I'm not even sure what I'm asking. I may not even remember this tomorrow."

"It's okay," he says back. Softly.

What did I ever do to deserve such a good friend?

Just when I think he can't surprise me anymore, he hits me with, "How about we talk tomorrow? We'll both be sober. We can set some ground rules."

"Ground rules?"

"For . . ." He falters, only for a second. "Whatever this is. Or whatever this could be."

"Okay. That sounds good."

"Good. Talk to you tomorrow, Keat. Get some sleep."

"You too," I say, and we hang up.

Penny opens one eye, as if to say, *What have you done now, human?*

"I have no idea," I mutter. This could be the most humiliating thing I've ever gotten myself into.

But then, without warning, I find myself grinning. Drunk grinning, which isn't necessarily my best look, but I wonder if Slate is grinning too.

If anything, this is definitely going to be interesting.

CHAPTER Two

Slate

FOR A MOMENT AFTER MY ALARM GOES OFF, I wonder if last night's conversation with Keaton was just some bizarre dream. But her words are right there in my text message history. *How about you stop making jokes and help me become a better lover?*

And then my not-so-eloquent response . . . *You want me to teach you how to fuck?*

I wince a little at the exchange, but then decide it doesn't matter. I've always been 100 percent myself around Keaton, which includes my lack of filter, and I'm certainly not about to change now. Not after a solid ten years of friendship. She obviously accepts me as I am, crass and all.

I shave, shower, and dress on autopilot, trying not to overthink it. There's no point jumping the gun here. We need to sit down and hash this out before we do anything else. But I still can't stop myself from puzzling over her.

Keaton didn't react well when I tried to confirm exactly what kind of help she was after. But I'm not crazy for interpreting things that way . . . right? Did she just want me to buy her a textbook or something? Draw her some X-rated diagrams? Demonstrate using a banana and a condom? No, I'm pretty sure she was talking about a more hands-on kind of instruction. Then again, maybe it was her liquid courage talking and she won't remember a damn thing.

Yet I can't deny that her indecent proposal excites me. She's stunning, like a sexy librarian fantasy come to life. Let's face it, I'm a red-blooded man with a functioning set of eyeballs who just so happens to have the equipment that can take care of whatever her needs require. No one could fault me for finding the idea of touching her appealing. If she wants me to be her personal love machine, let's face it, I'll jump at the chance.

But we're just friends—always have been, and hopefully always will be. I know she's married to her job, and she knows I'm not interested in settling down. Neither of us wants to fuck up all the good things we've got going on, especially not our friendship.

I tell myself firmly that there's no way any of the images playing through my mind are going to come true. Whatever she meant last night, she's probably come to her senses by now. Or she might have been too drunk for the memory to stick in the first place. I have to prepare myself for anything, including politely pretending to have forgotten in case she's embarrassed at what Drunk Keaton said. God knows she's afforded me the same courtesy plenty of times when I said something stupid while drinking.

I text Keaton to let her know I'm on my way, and she answers with a thumbs-up emoji. Not exactly a "Roger that, I'm ready to talk about fucking," but she's probably still waking up. I just wanted to make sure I didn't walk in on her naked . . . no, thinking about Naked Keaton is the absolute wrong way to go here.

Just turn off your brain, put away your phone, and get in the car, Slate.

On my way to her place, I swing by Keaton's favorite breakfast spot to pick up a couple of their famous giant breakfast burritos with extra cheese. She's not a big drinker, and knowing her, she's probably not feeling great. So I need to get some food in her to soak up the after-effects of that bachelorette party.

I take the elevator up to her apartment and ring

the doorbell. She answers my buzz in a pair of pink pajama pants, a T-shirt, and bare feet. Her long dark hair is bundled into a messy ponytail, but somehow she still looks put together.

I can't help but wonder if the bright smile on her face is for me, and my lips twitch in amusement.

"Morning," I say, holding out the paper bag to Keaton as I step inside. I can't resist adding, "Nice outfit."

"Thanks." She takes my offering and inhales the spicy aroma with a rapturous sigh. "Oh God, I can smell the green chilis. So good."

"I thought you might need a hangover cure."

Her cat, Penny, glares down at the disturbance from her perch on top of the refrigerator.

I shut the door behind me before Penny can get out. Not that such an old, curmudgeonly cat can be bothered to move that fast, but Keaton would die if that damn cat ever escaped.

"I didn't drink *quite* that much last night, but thank you." She puts the bag on the kitchen table. "Let me make us some coffee. Can you get the plates?"

"Right after I greet Penny." I walk to the fridge and reach up to stroke the grizzled orange tabby. "Hey there, girl, how's Penny the Punisher?"

She doesn't move, barely tolerating my gesture of affection.

"It's so weird how well she gets along with you," Keaton comments from over by the coffee machine.

"Hey, that hurts. I like to think I'm a pretty likable guy." I scratch Penny's fluffy cheek, and she favors me with a slow blink of her half-lidded green eyes.

My focus is on Keaton, though, trying to decipher if she remembers any of our conversation last night. But she doesn't let on, doesn't give me any indication if I'm likable enough for the bedroom activities she wants help with. I still have no idea if I'm a candidate for the job.

"You know what I mean." Keaton rolls her eyes. "She barely even lets me pet her. And whenever she's on top of the fridge like this . . . well, just watch."

Keaton leans past me to open the fridge—so close I can feel her body heat and catch a whiff of her lavender shampoo—and reaches for the milk carton. Lightning-fast, Penny swats the top of her head.

Keaton widens her eyes at me in exaggerated disbelief. "See?"

I suppress a laugh. "I don't call her Penny the Punisher for nothing."

"Well, I know she's just playing. Otherwise, she'd use her claws."

She's a little delusional about her cat, but I'm not going to correct her. That cat is a mean old thing who only needs humans for one thing: food.

Keaton pours us two steaming cups of coffee, one black for her, and another with a healthy splash of milk for me.

As I stir a spoonful of sugar into my coffee at the table, her open laptop catches my eye, and I do an involuntary double-take. A spreadsheet is on the screen . . . but not filled with dry financial data like I expected. It's a long list of lewd acts, from *blow-job basics* and *new positions* to *dirty talk* and *anal*, all meticulously sorted with color-coded tabs.

Holy shit, it's a sex syllabus. I almost choke on my scalding-hot drink.

Okay, well, um . . . she clearly hasn't forgotten last night. And I guess that's one way to go about learning. A very organized, very Keaton way. I'm caught between shock and laughter.

What should I do? Sure, I came over here so we could talk about Keaton's sex life, but I don't know if this spreadsheet is something I was supposed to see. Maybe she made it for her, uh, private use. Trying to pretend I didn't read the screen, I turn the laptop away and scoot it aside to make room for our plates, and almost knock it off the table in guilty surprise when the doorbell buzzes.

Keaton answers the door to a tiny white-haired old Indian woman. She holds out a plastic measuring cup.

"Sorry to bother you so early, dear. I just wanted to borrow some sugar." Her voice is soft and heavily accented.

Smiling, Keaton waves her hand. "It's no trouble at all. I'll grab the canister and you can take as much as you need."

This must be her neighbor she's told me about, but I've never met.

As Keaton goes to rummage around in her pantry, the old woman spots me and touches her cheek in consternation. "Oh dear, I'm interrupting. I didn't realize you had a . . . guest. Who is this handsome gentleman?"

"This is my friend Slate. He just brought over some breakfast for us to share." Keaton emerges with a small canister of sugar and starts pouring it into the old woman's cup, maybe a little faster than necessary.

Is it just me, or did she emphasize the word *friend*? And make extra effort to imply that I didn't spend the night?

"How sweet of him." The woman's wrinkles crease deeper in a fond smile. "You two would make a cute couple."

"'Bye, Meera." Keaton's reply is gentle but firm. "I'll see you for tea on Sunday at two."

Once the door is shut, Keaton sits down at the kitchen table and unwraps her burrito with a sigh. "Sorry about that. Meera's always after me to 'find a nice man and settle down.' Her kids don't call or visit much, so I guess I get the brunt of her hovering."

"No problem. She seems like a nice lady."

I take a bite of my burrito, and for a while, we just concentrate on eating in comfortable silence.

When my plate is half-empty, I say, "So, about the . . ." I search for the right word, then decide *fuck it, just cut to the chase.* "The sex thing. Tell me what you're thinking."

Keaton stops chewing for a second, then swallows. "Right. Well," she says slowly, "it's like I said last night. I don't have sex skills, and I want to change that."

"But why is this bothering you so much? I don't get what the big deal is. I'm sure you're just fine in bed—"

"Because I feel like I've missed out, Slate. There's all this fun everyone else got to have while I was concentrating on climbing the corporate ladder. It's like I've sacrificed a huge part of my life to the gods of software sales." She looks aside, down at the linoleum.

Shit, I didn't realize how sensitive she was about this. Usually Keaton is so no-nonsense, so rarely ashamed of anything . . . No, this isn't quite like shame. It's more like bitterness. Sadness. Coupled with the no-nonsense confidence she has about tackling any problem in her path.

I put down my burrito to show her she has my full attention. "Sorry. I didn't mean to imply your feelings were wrong; I was just trying to understand why you were so upset. And I really hope you don't think less of yourself just because you didn't suck off some stupid cucumber the right way at a party while everyone was watching. You're an amazing person, Keaton, and you've accomplished so much."

She snorts. "When you put it that way, my problem sounds even dumber. And I did suck it off, just really crappily."

Man, I'm really hitting it out of the park here. "Never mind. Let's start over." I fold my hands on the table. "Let's get back to your goals. What exactly do you want to learn, and how are you going to approach it?"

Maybe if I put things in more of a business-language way, it'll make it easier for her to get her thoughts together.

She nods to herself, then glances at her laptop. "Well, I *was* working on something last night, just to try organizing . . ." Before I can figure out what to say about the dirty list, she trails off into hesitation, chewing her lip. "But first—listen, I don't want to put you in an impossible situation. I know we're friends, and I'd never want to ruin that, so please don't think you have to do anything with me just because I got drunk and whiny."

I put up my hands to stop her. "Hey, it's all good. We're cool." I knew this backpedaling was coming, but I still can't help feeling slightly disappointed. "How about this—what if I could be your wingman? Help you find the right guy to practice with?"

She blinks. "You'd do that for me?"

"Of course. You're my friend." I reach across the table to squeeze her shoulder. "Besides, you've helped me get laid tons of times. Even if this wasn't so important to you, it'd be only fair for me to return the favor."

"First, you've never needed help getting laid, Slate. You walk into a room and girls practically throw their panties at you. And second, I think this could be a great idea." She grins at me, her deep blue eyes sparkling. "Thank you so much. When can we start?"

"I'm free tonight if you are. We can hit up the new nightclub that just opened up on Butler Street." I find their website on my phone and show it to her.

She studies the photos of featured DJs and neon-lit, scantily clad crowds, her eyes narrowing as she assesses the scene. "That soon?"

I shrug. "Why not? No time like the present."

A familiar determination comes over her heart-shaped face. I know that look well. Once Keaton has set her mind to something, she never backs down.

I smile, amused at her resolve. "Then I'll meet you there at nine."

"Thanks, Slate." She grins at me again.

"Oh, and Keaton—wear something sexy."

Her eyes widen, and then she bites her lip and gives me a determined nod like the good little student she is.

CHAPTER
Three

Keaton

THE DRESS I'M WEARING IS ONE KARINA PICKED out for me on our last retail-therapy binge. In the reflection of the bar window, I quickly examine the curves the little raspberry-colored dress shows off.

The silken material of the bodice climbs all the way up to my collarbone, but a slit down the center reveals just enough cleavage to say, "Hello!" The sleeves are three-quarter length, made of a tight, stretchy lace material. With the slight elevation of shoulder pads hidden under the seams, I look like I stepped off a women's fashion magazine boasting, "Darling or dangerous?"

"Oh, Mama!" Karina said, doing her best husky man-voice as I twirled in front of her in the dressing room several weeks ago.

"You sure it's not too . . . I don't know, CEO?" I

asked, poking at the slight padding on my shoulder.

"It's CE-*Oh, Mama!* There's a difference." Karina smirked, and I bought it immediately.

Now, standing outside the bar where I'll be putting this little outfit to the test, I feel slightly less confident. I crack open my clutch purse—black, simple, with small studs embellishing the corners—and pull out my phone.

I'm outside the bar. Where are you?

I press SEND, my fingers clumsy with nervous energy. I don't know if Slate has arrived and is already inside. I don't want to walk in alone. How is it possible that I can be so confident walking in the office every morning but then completely lose my shit outside a run-of-the-mill bar? I squint through the window, trying to make out Slate's familiar silhouette against the dozens of people moving around inside, but I don't spot him.

Almost there. The driver got
turned around. Just go in.

I groan. Of course Slate would say that. He's so cool and confident; he probably thinks this is no big deal.

Nervous, I lick my lips. Instantly regretting it, I un-click my clutch purse again and fish around for my lip-stick. If there's one thing I've gotten good at as a highly ambitious woman in a predominantly male field, it's knowing my lipsticks. Colors matter, if not within the mess of stupid gender politics, then for my own level of confidence. The typical nudes and blushes I wear to work are tucked safely away in my vanity back at home. Tonight, Blood Berry is my weapon of choice.

The sweet and sexy color glides over my lips with ease. As I lean into the reflection of the window to make sure my lips are perfect, I spot a man on the other side of the glass watching me from the bar. He smiles, giving me a thumbs-up. I blush but smile back. His face is suddenly obscured by another re-flection. I nearly jump out of my skin at the closeness of Slate's voice in my ear.

"Looks like you've started without me. You sure you need a wingman?"

The deep, rich voice almost seems to vibrate through me. I turn and punch him on the arm, but he doesn't even flinch. Admittedly, I'm more grateful that he's here than I am pissed that he startled me.

"You freaking scared me." I laugh, catching my breath.

Slate grins, and we both look at each other, taking in the other's choice of clothes. Slate is dressed business casual, wearing a dark gray dress shirt with the sleeves rolled up, the top button undone to show off a hint of his toned chest and handsome Adam's apple. His slacks are a perfect fit, hugging his muscular legs in all the right places, ending sleekly at the charmingly scuffed dress shoes on his feet.

He looks good. I notice that he's checking me out, as well. His gaze trails from my neck, where I've pushed my hair aside, all the way to my cleavage. I swallow, hit by a sudden wave of nerves.

"Yeah?" I ask, doing the same timid twirl I did for Karina when I first tried it on.

"Yeah," he says, his gaze still on my cleavage. He clears his throat. "I mean—yeah, it's good."

"Seriously? It's *good*? Fuck." I throw my hands up in frustration. "It's too much, as usual. Am I overdressed for this bar?"

"No, Keat, no." Slate places his hands on my fidgeting arms, his touch immediately steadying me. "You're fucking perfect. I'm going to look like a total schmuck next to you."

I blush, letting the compliment blossom over my cheeks. "Well, good thing I'm the focus of tonight, right?" I wink at him, and he looks away abruptly.

What was that about?

"Yup, good thing," he says, recovering. "Now, let's get you in there and find a nice, wholesome gentleman for you to fuck into next week."

He props open the door, and the music inside wafts out to us. Slate ushers me inside and pays the cover charge for both of us. I make a mental note to pay him back. Just because he's helping me score doesn't mean he should pay for everything.

We walk up to the bar to get a drink. Slate pulls out a stool for me, and I sit while he leans against the bar. While we wait for the bartender to notice us, I begin surveying the merchandise. There are a lot of viable candidates in this bar.

Slate was right . . . this spot was a good place to start. Not too crowded, not too trashy. Just the right amount of single men winding down after a long week, looking for a little fun. My gaze wanders as I take in the prospects.

"My God, they aren't cattle," Slate whispers.

I turn to him with a scowl and lean back immediately. He was much closer to me than I thought, close enough that I can count each of his enviably dark and full eyelashes. It's these little details that soften his chiseled angles in a way that's so alluring.

Did I seriously just use the word alluring *to*

describe Slate? Jesus, Keaton.

Maybe I really do need to get laid worse than I thought.

"I'm looking at my options," I say, defending myself with a bit of a bite to my voice. The typical Slate-and-Keaton banter is cutting a little deeper than it usually does. I'm trying to put myself out there tonight, and it's proving to be harder than I thought.

"How about we get some drinks before we make them battle it out for you?"

I nod, my mouth pinched tight.

"Hey, hey. Chin up. That's what the alcohol is for." Slate flags down the bartender.

A cute twenty-something woman with tattoos and an asymmetrical haircut sidles up to us, ready to take our order. "What can I get you?" she says with a stupidly attractive smile.

"Vodka soda, please," Slate replies with his equally stupid and attractive smile. "Heavy on the vodka."

"Lemon or lime?"

"Both."

She laughs, watching him with twinkling eyes.

"Keat?" he says, gesturing to me.

The bartender notices me for the first time as her gaze swings over to land on me.

"A whiskey and Coke for me, please. Thank you."

"You got it." She nods.

Does she think I'm Slate's girlfriend? Weirdly, I don't mind her making that mistake. I don't want him dating someone in that experimental-hairstyle phase anyway. If she doesn't know what she wants to wear on her head, how in the hell does she know what she wants in her bed? I was in her shoes once, and I was a mess.

"Classic Keaton. You can order a flirty cocktail for once, you know. Something actually enjoyable?" Slate teases me.

"Yeah? Should I get a lemon *and* a lime in it too? Seems like someone can't make a decision," I tease back, raising my eyebrows in challenge.

"My drinks reflect my complicated heart," he says with a melodramatic sigh.

"Oh my God, Slate, you are the furthest thing from complicated." I place a hand on his cheek, and he grins at me.

"Guilty."

We stand like that for a moment, smiling at each other, my hand resting on his sharp jawline in a gesture that may violate the platonic playing field. As if he can read my mind, Slate turns away and my hand slips from his face.

The bartender drops off our drinks, and Slate

hands her his card with a suggestion to keep the tab running. His gaze drops to her ass as she turns to help another customer.

I jab him hard in the ribs. "Focus," I remind him. "Tonight is about me."

"Right, right. Anyone interest you?"

I follow his gaze as it turns to the multitude of eligible males in the room and take in my options. "I don't know. The first thing on my list is practicing my blow-job technique."

Slate seems to sputter at my choice of words—put so matter-of-factly.

I grin and press on. "What kind of guys should I be looking for?"

The look on his face makes me wonder if I sprouted a second nose between my eyes.

"Literally any man in this room would be honored to introduce his dick to you, Keaton. Let's focus a little less on the list and a little more on what kind of guy you *want* to blow."

"Okay, okay." I look around the room.

There's a tall guy in the back, surrounded by other guy friends. Black curly hair, broad chest, big smile. He laughs uproariously at something one of them says.

Cute, but a lot to handle, I bet.

My gaze shifts to the quieter corners of the room. Maybe someone with a little less of a presence. Someone who will be easygoing about this whole thing. Someone chill. Because that's what I need.

I spot a guy sitting by the door. Brown hair, brown eyes, the right amount of scruff. Sleeves rolled up, just the way I like. He looks to be part of a big group, talking here and there to people in passing, but never dominating the conversation. I like him already.

"That one," I say, pointing to him.

I immediately regret the gesture because the man's gaze flicks to me in alarm, spotting my eagle eye on him. I whip around toward the bar in my catastrophic embarrassment.

"Oh my God," I whimper. Well, this is already fucked.

"Yup, very smooth. He's on his way over. Good luck, champ."

Slate is about to turn away when I grab his hand discreetly, so no one else can see.

"What do I say?" My voice is so pathetic, I want to hurl myself out the bar window.

"Anything, Keat. Just think of this as a trial run. He's not the only guy you'll talk to tonight."

Slate gives my hand a subtle squeeze before

scooting away to wave down the bartender for another drink. I watch him leave me behind, my breath caught in my throat.

"Is there something on my face?" a voice says from behind me.

I turn slowly, gathering myself, and smile at the man before me. "Just a lot of handsome?"

Goddammit. That was so very bad.

The man smiles warmly, though, and I feel slightly less like a failure.

"That's very kind of you," he says, offering his hand. "James."

"Keaton," I reply. "I'm not good at this."

"It was a little forward, yes, but I like forward."

Shit. He's got the wrong idea about me. Or does he? Aren't I trying to get this guy in my bed? Let's be forward.

"Forward it is, then." I flash my best saleswoman smile that I usually save for my most desired clients. "Tell me about yourself, James."

I don't expect the tidal wave that crashes over me when I open the conversation.

James is an engineer, but a performer at heart. He's also in an improvisation group that performs every other Tuesday at this very bar, and I should *totally come!* He has a brother visiting next weekend who doesn't believe in having artistic outlets, which is absurd to James since he thinks Improv is what keeps him sane. (Improv is capitalized by the way James says it.) James has a dog named Buck who does his share of keeping James busy with all the vet fees he's had to pay. "Worms," he says, "it's always stomach worms." He thinks I would like Buck, though, because Buck likes pretty ladies. Do I like dogs?

"Cats," I choke out, realizing it's finally my turn to speak. "I'm more of a cat lady, myself."

How did I horribly misjudge this chatterbox as an easygoing, never-dominating-the-conversation type? I'll never trust my gut ever again.

"Cats, huh? That says a lot about a woman."

"Does it?" I gulp, bracing myself for more of *The James Show.*

I find myself looking around for a live studio audience, or at least a few hidden cameras. Instead, I spot Slate, staring at us from down the bar. What's that on his face? Are those fucking tears of laughter? I shoot him the dirtiest look I can muster. He gives me a pitying look that says, *Okay, okay, here I come.*

"Cat ladies are unpredictable, in my experience. Last woman I was with—hey!" James cuts himself off as Slate puts a hand on my shoulder.

"Slate, honey!" I croon. "You *have* to meet my new friend, James. James, this is my very good friend Slate."

"Hello, handsome," Slate nearly purrs.

Oh, this is my *favorite* act. Now it's my turn to improvise, James.

"Isn't he?" I smile at the man but speak to Slate. "I can totally envision it, can't you?" I clasp Slate's hand in mine in an intimate gesture of companionship.

"Hello, uh, Slate?" James says, suddenly a bit speechless.

"Like the rock, baby." Slate winks at poor James, who is now turning a deep shade of crimson.

"What do you think, honey?" I whisper to Slate. "You like? You think he's your type too?"

Slate takes his time looking James up and down, considering, and I daresay he's added to his act by stepping behind James to take a gander at that part of the real estate, as well. But James doesn't give him a chance to confirm or deny.

"You know, uh, it's been lovely chatting with you, Katie," he stammers, and I grit my teeth behind my tight-lipped smile. "I should probably get back to my friends, though."

"Of course, Slate and I will totally make it to

your improv soon . . . 'bye," I say, waving James off. As soon as he scoots away, my cheery demeanor crumples.

"Just my damn luck," I say to Slate with a sigh, who places his arm around my shoulders. "I'm used to being mansplained in the office, but at the bar too?" I shudder.

Slate laughs and rubs my back in a gesture of comfort. My icy mood melts at his touch and I lean into his side, enjoying his warmth and support. What did I ever do to deserve such a great wingman?

"Don't worry, *Katie*. We'll find you a nice guy who won't talk your little ears off . . . and one who loves cats too."

He yanks on my earlobe and a jolt of energy passes through me, covering my arms and legs in faint goose bumps. *That was unexpected.*

"What about that guy over there? He's been eyeing you."

I follow his gaze to a man sitting with a small group of friends in a booth. Blond hair, cropped short to his head. Glasses and a nice sweater. Cute and clean cut. Not exactly my type, but when our eyes meet and he smiles invitingly, my heart skips a little. I smile back.

"See?" Slate says. "Let's go get you a blow job, buddy."

I laugh under my breath, and together we walk over to the booth. "You lead this time?"

"Sure," he says.

Immediately, I feel safe and a thousand times more confident. This is Slate's domain, here in the bustling bar scene. It isn't mine, and I don't need to pretend it is.

Slate will help me. That's why he's here, right?

CHAPTER
Four

Slate

AS KEATON FOLLOWS ME OVER TO THE TABLE where Blond Glasses Guy sits, I take quick stock of its occupants: our target, plus one man and two women, nobody sitting close enough to each other to suggest any sort of romantic connection.

So he has female friends. I add a point to my mental scoreboard. A low bar, I know, but I've met a depressing number of guys in my time who didn't clear it. This at least suggests that he sees women as more than conquests.

"Excuse me," I say to announce our approach, and Blond Glasses Guy looks up. "I couldn't help but notice you were checking out my friend here."

Flustered, he blinks rapidly, his gaze flicking between me and Keaton. "Oh, sorry, I didn't mean to bother you."

I laugh. He probably thinks I'm here to start a fight. "Actually, she was the opposite of bothered. I thought we'd come over and introduce ourselves. I'm Slate, and this is Keaton."

"Hi," Keaton says, almost shyly. It's strange—and kind of cute—to see her acting so different from her usual take-charge attitude.

"I'm Greg." He stands up to shake her hand first, and then mine. Good manners . . . another point in his favor.

The two women at the table giggle and whisper to each other. The other man cracks a smile that's almost lost in his bushy beard.

Greg grins sheepishly. "Would you like to sit down?" he asks, making sure to address both of us.

Polite, not too pushy. Potentially a positive, to put Keaton's skittishness at ease, but if she loses her nerve and can't make the first move, he might just let things fizzle out. I'll have to keep an eye on the situation.

"Really? You don't mind if we join you?" Keaton looks like she can't believe her luck.

One of the women pipes up. "Not at all. I'm Abby, by the way. And this is Sofia and Ethan."

I don't miss the appreciative eye Abby gives me.

Keaton sits gingerly next to Greg, like she's

trying to perch on a land mine without exploding it. This is so not like Keaton, and I'm not sure what to make of it.

Sofia says something in an undertone, and Ethan snorts.

Abby leans toward me, a generous glimpse of tanned cleavage peeking out from her loose gold blouse. "So, what do you do?"

I turn to face her, but behind me, I can hear Greg and Keaton starting a fumbling yet earnest conversation. "I'm a sports agent. I negotiate contracts for athletes and communicate with their team owners, managers, and coaches, that sort of thing."

"Wow, that is so awesome!" Abby squeals. "Have you met any really famous people?"

"Quite a few." I flash her my patented panty-melting smile. "But right now, my friend and I are just out looking for a good time. What—"

"—do you do?" I overhear Greg asking Keaton.

"I work in software sales," Keaton says, her voice chipper. It's cute how she loves her job.

"What a coincidence. I'm actually a programmer, myself."

I stiffen, waiting for him to mansplain her own job to her—another problem I've seen way too many times.

But instead, he asks, "What do you think of Java?"

"Oh Christ, fucking Java." Keaton groans, and they both laugh.

"What were you saying?" Abby prompts me.

Sofia and Ethan have already started their own side conversation, something about a dumb customer at the coffee shop where he works.

"Uh . . ." I forgot. Oh, right. "How about you?" I try to shut out Greg and Keaton's words and get back on track.

"I work at an art gallery. So I answer the phone, manage the budget, coordinate events, liaise with artists . . ." Abby chuckles and rests her hand on my arm. "That last part is a little bit like what you do with athletes, I guess. Or am I wrong?"

"Infiniti Key specializes in security and encryption software, doesn't it?" Greg asks.

"That's right. I'm surprised you've even heard of my company." Keaton sounds impressed.

"I like to stay informed about local businesses. It's kind of a hobby," Greg replies.

I want to roll my eyes a little. *Oh, come on, man, there's no way you can say something like that without sounding douchey.* But Keaton still looks as rapt as ever, so I try to chalk it up to different strokes for different folks.

"Did you hear me?" Abby says a little testily.

I yank my attention back to her. "Sorry. Do you like to paint yourself? Uh, not like that avant-garde thing—" *Shut the hell up!* "—where you get naked and cover yourself in body paint. I meant paint on paper. Canvas."

Jesus fucking Christ, what's wrong with me?

"Yeah," Abby says slowly. "I do. I'm hoping to get good enough to take commissions. Although, I actually work with digital media, not traditional."

"That's really neat. What kind of subjects do you like to draw?" I ask.

I don't hear her answer because Keaton cracks up, and I involuntarily glance over at her. Abby's fuchsia-painted lips pinch together.

Dammit . . . she's getting frustrated, and I don't blame her. What happened to my game tonight? Normally, I'd be all over such a cute, cool, obviously interested girl, but I keep dropping the ball. I'm not even trying to eavesdrop, but fucking Greg is still making me miss all my cues.

I take another few stabs at chatting with Abby and the rest of the table. Making a good impression on Greg's friends can only help Keaton score.

But all my small talk falls flat; Greg and Keaton's

chattering is just too distracting. Resigning myself to looking antisocial, I let the others get back to whatever they were talking about before we showed up. I turn my ear to the lovebirds, ready to jump in if Keaton needs a helping hand.

But it seems like she's got everything under control.

"So then the guy asks me if this product is compatible with their COBOL system, and I almost piss my pants," Keaton says.

Greg grimaces in playful sympathy. "Oh jeez, I'm so sorry. Lawyers, am I right?"

"I know! Thank God I was on the phone and he couldn't see my face. I was just like . . ." She raises her voice to her perky customer-service tone. "Um, I'm afraid not, but I can recommend some other vendors to you."

"Ouch. Sorry you lost the sale. Still, I wish I had your quick thinking . . . would've come in handy with last month's client from hell." He rubs the back of his neck. "But, uh, you probably don't want to hear about that."

"Actually, I love funny client stories. I mean, we've all got one." She sips her drink.

"True." He beams at her, and I frown. *Okay, dude, you can dial down the googly eyes.* "Man . . . you're really cool. I'm glad we ran into each other tonight."

It's hard to tell in the dim light, but I think Keaton's cheeks turn pink. "Really?"

He scoots toward her a tiny bit. "I hope I'm not being too forward."

"No, no, it's fine. Actually, you can be even more forward if you want. My mantra tonight has been 'forward, it is.'" She grins, biting her lip adorably, and I repress the urge to throw something.

I try to stop listening, but I can't, and my mood sours more with every enthralled word.

Greg. Ugh, of course he's a Greg. A generic name for a painfully generic guy.

I knock back another slug of my drink. No wonder he feels like he has to make up for his boring personality with that tacky-ass hipster sweater. Who the hell wears a sweater to a nightclub, anyway? He looks like somebody's colorblind grandpa. And when did my glass empty? And . . .

Why is his stupid face bugging me so much?

I excuse myself—not that anyone notices—under the pretext of ordering another drink, but really to cool off and figure out where this bad taste in my mouth is coming from.

Initially, I thought Greg was such a great choice for her. This whole thing was my idea in the first place, wasn't it? We came here to get Keaton laid, it's my job to help her, and it looks like we're making great progress on that front. So, why doesn't it feel like a success to see them click so well?

"You want a refill?" a female voice shouts over the thumping music.

"Huh?" I look up to see the same tattooed bartender who served us when we first came in.

"Vodka soda with lemon and lime, wasn't it?" she asks.

"Oh. Yeah, that's right, thanks. You have a good memory." I'll have to give her a hefty tip when we finally cash out.

She winks. "Only for the pretty ones," she says, and I don't even acknowledge her reply.

What the fuck is wrong with me? Any other night, I'd be all over this chick like white on rice. Tonight, though? Scoring is the furthest thing from my mind.

While she makes my drink, I keep watching the table out of the corner of my eye. Even all the way over by the bar, where I can't hear their amazing, chemistry-laden chatter anymore, I can still tell they're hitting it off.

Keaton laughs—not a fake polite titter, but with her mouth open wide and her nose slightly wrinkled, in the way she only does when she's genuinely having a good time. Greg brushes a stray hair out of her face, and I want to slap his hand away.

I breathe a sigh of relief when she gets up and heads toward the restroom.

It finally occurs to me that the bartender was flirting. Even if it was only to get a bigger tip and not out of any sort of real desire, I still should have said something back. Shit, I'm seriously losing my cool here. I force myself to turn around and stop spying like a nutcase.

What the hell does Keaton see in Greg? He's not that good-looking. From what I overheard of the conversation, he's not that interesting either. Keaton can do way better. She *deserves* better.

Yeah, that must be it . . . I'm just sensing something off about the guy. My douche-radar is tingling. I'm subconsciously looking out for her best interests, that's all.

I'm in such a hurry, I almost forget to thank the bartender when she hands over my drink. I weave my way back through the crowd to Greg's table and lean in so he can hear me.

"Hey, listen, buddy . . . sorry, but tonight's gonna be a no-go."

Greg blinks like an owl behind those big glasses. "Why?"

"Uh . . ." Dammit, I didn't think that far ahead. I just want this guy to give up the chase. I blurt out the first excuse that pops into my vodka-fuzzed brain. "Diarrhea."

He gives me a weird look. "What?"

Too late to backpedal now. Gotta roll with it. "She had wicked diarrhea earlier. If she's been in the bathroom that long, I'm guessing her bowels must be flaring up again."

His face screws up in disgust. "Oh," he mutters. "Well, thanks for the warning, I guess."

"No problem. Sorry things didn't work out in your favor tonight."

I'm not remotely sorry about that. What I am sorry for is throwing Keaton under the irritable-bowel bus to do it. I didn't mean to get quite so personal—I just panicked.

With a good-bye to his friends, Greg gets up and heads out.

Keaton approaches a few minutes later. Her walk slows to a stop and her smile wilts. She looks around, her expression morphing from confused to crestfallen as she realizes her suitor has ditched her, and my stomach clenches like I've swallowed hot ashes.

Fuck. I did this to her. Guilt washes over me, making my stomach pitch.

I saved her, I try to tell myself. That dude was all wrong for her. I mean, if a guy can't handle the idea of a woman needing to use the bathroom, he's not worth my best friend's time anyway. Right?

Then why do I suddenly feel like such an asshole?

I head over to join her, the crowd partially screening us from Greg's friends. She looks at me with huge blue eyes and downturned crimson lips. *God, I'm being such an asshole right now.*

"Did I say something wrong?" she asks in a crushed undertone.

"No, of course not. You could never say anything that bad. He just had to get going all of a sudden. I don't know, maybe he has an early morning tomorrow." *Stop babbling, Slate.* I take a deep breath. "He . . . seemed like he really liked you."

Keaton's brow creases. "Then why not at least get my phone number before he bailed?" A sharper note has entered her voice—so sharp that it's as angry and bewildered as I feel.

I shrug helplessly. "I don't know. Clearly, he's an idiot. Come on, I'll buy you another drink and we can try again."

With a comforting hand on her shoulder, I walk her away from Greg's table and back to the bar. Even my lingering guilt can't drown out the relief I feel.

"I can't believe I struck out every single time," Keaton says with a whine. "I tried all night and not one goddamn penis wanted me to touch it. God, my fucking feet hurt so bad."

I loop my arm around her waist, partially to comfort her and partially to hold her up as we stagger down the sidewalk to her apartment. It's almost two in the morning, and the streets are deserted. Only the predawn stars are watching over us.

"Don't think of it as striking out. Think of it as . . ." I wave my hand, searching for a positive spin. "Being selective. You just didn't meet a good match, and it's better to go home alone than with the wrong guy."

She growls loudly in frustration. "I'm not looking for a friggin' husband; I'm just trying to get laid! There's no point in being picky. Face it, Slate, it's not me who has the high standards here. Guys just don't like me. End of story."

I stop in my tracks. "That's not true."

She sways in my arms to face me with tipsy defiance. "Really? Because literally everything that happened tonight says different."

"So you had one bad night? Big deal. Plenty of

guys like you."

"Prove it," she insists, her eyes brimming with need and wounded pride.

Her body is so warm, her scent so sweet, and it all feels perfectly natural to just lean in and . . .

Our lips meet. She squeaks in surprise, but before I can pull away and apologize, she kisses me back. *Hard.*

Her hot, soft mouth crushes against mine, opening with an intense hunger, her tongue demanding entrance, and I can't help devouring her right back. I couldn't stop, even if I wanted to.

Why the hell haven't I done this before? What have I been missing out on all these years?

All my reservations and doubts are swept away in a wave of desire. No overthinking, no self-doubt, just chemistry. Pure, primal instinct. Our tongues touch and my heart rate triples because, holy fuck . . . I'm kissing my best friend.

And, fuck me, I really, really like it.

We break the kiss, both flushed and breathing a little harder, a powerful new tension buzzing between us. Goddamn . . . just that one moment of contact was enough to send every drop of blood traveling from my brain straight to my dick.

Keaton's never given me wood, not even once.

Okay, that's a lie. There was this one time that she rubbed my shoulders and her boob brushed my arm by accident, but that was just biology. That's all that was.

"That was . . ." I pause.

It should have felt weird, like kissing my sister. I've always had a strictly platonic relationship with Keaton. But I can't lie. It was perfect. Like a textbook-perfect kiss, chemistry and attraction, and just the right amount of tongue. And I want to do it again as soon as possible.

"Yeah," Keaton murmurs. Her gaze has darkened. She licks her lips and glances up at her apartment building. "Want to come inside?"

CHAPTER
Five

Keaton

A S I ENTER MY APARTMENT AHEAD OF SLATE, my head is buzzing with alcohol, questions, and a heaping dose of *holy shit*.

What was that kiss? Besides *amazing*, a little voice inside my head whispers. That was definitely not a gesture between friends.

It was sweet, hot, and so natural. But also totally unexpected. In all the years I've been friends with Slate, our relationship has always been strictly platonic.

I wish I could read the look on his face right now. He shrugs off his jacket, and I'm about to open my mouth to break this unbearable silence when a loud meowing begins. The patter of small paws on the wooden floor of my front hall draws our attention to Penny, ambling toward us with demands for attention.

"Hello, sweetness," Slate says, his voice warm, and Penny purrs immediately. He crouches down before the orange fluff-muffin, offering the back of his hand for her to rub against.

I watch in amazement. *Traitor. See if he'll be the one who feeds you.*

"Well, aren't you a lover," he murmurs. Amazingly, Penny has rolled over so her belly is exposed. He runs one of his beautiful hands gently across her downy fur, and she makes a purring noise.

"What sort of voodoo magic is this?" I mutter. "Are you a cat whisperer? She'll never let me do this."

"Not at all." He smirks. "Penny just knows who here has the magic touch."

"Magic touch?" I roll my eyes.

He shrugs. "Take it up with Penny."

We both fall silent for a few moments. I can't stop thinking about exactly how magic the touch of his lips felt against mine. There's a joke on the tip of my tongue—and I consider asking him if his magic touch is exclusive to domesticated animals, or does it extend to their sexually frustrated owners too?

Instead, I clear my throat. "I should feed the monster. She'll try to eat your hand before long."

"I'll help," he says.

I lead him into the kitchen, where I prepare

Penny's food, but not too much since it's late and she's already fat enough. Penny digs in, flecks of wet cat food catching on her whiskers.

"Not so sweet now, are you?" I say, observing her manners in front of our guest, and Slate laughs. I love the sound of his laugh. It's rich and deep, and I want to hear more of it. "Do you want a beer?" I ask him after a moment of comfortable silence between us.

"Sure," he says.

He's leaning against the fridge in a bizarrely sexy way, one foot lazily crossed in front of the other. I find myself staring at how his arms fold over his broad chest, emphasizing the size of his biceps. Have they always been that nicely defined?

I take a step toward him. He doesn't move, comfortable where he is, comfortable with me stepping into his personal space.

"Typically, one keeps beer chilled in the fridge," I say in a low voice, a gentle hint for him to step aside and let me open the door.

"I've heard that as well," he says with a cheeky angle to his smile.

We're only inches apart now. My hand rests on the door handle, my fingers grazing the edge of his shirtsleeve.

"So, maybe you should move?" I tug gently at his sleeve.

He eyes my fingers with a smile. "Make me, Keaton," he says, and my heart starts to pump faster.

There's nothing casual about the way my lips find his again in a hungry search for answers. His mouth opens against mine, and it feels just as right as it did outside.

I've never allowed myself to imagine how Slate might kiss, which is probably a good thing because this defies all logic. His lips are demanding, yet soft, and when his tongue sweeps against mine, I find it difficult to remain upright.

The warmth of his hands moves to my waist, and he pulls me closer against him. I lean in, wanting more. It's been a long time since I've been touched so intimately, and a pleasant ache spreads south.

"Sorry," I say with a nervous laugh when we finally part, both of us breathless.

"Don't apologize," he murmurs, his voice low and sensual.

His hands are still wrapped around my waist, and I'm struck by how large and sure they feel against me—a fact I've never noticed before. Wordless now, we stand with our chests pressed intimately against each other.

I realize that my hands are resting on his shoulders. I've felt them before, once when I gave him a completely innocent shoulder rub. But this feels entirely different. He's so sturdy, I just want to melt against him.

"Keaton . . ." He's staring at my lips.

"Yeah?" And now I'm staring at his.

"This is happening," he says, his eyes flashing confidently on mine. "Are you okay with that?"

My gaze lifts from his lips to his eyes. The most gorgeous shade of golden brown stares back at me.

"I don't know what this means. Do we just forget the whole wingman idea and . . . go for it?" When he doesn't answer for a moment, I pull back slightly, suddenly self-conscious. "What?"

He senses my nervousness and plants a kiss on my forehead. It radiates warmth throughout my whole body.

"Let's crack open those beers," he says with a reassuring smile.

One and then two beers are popped open and we each take a swig. I put some distance between us and sit on the counter. Slate sits on one of my metallic counter stools, his hands wrapped contemplatively around his drink.

Penny is done with her meal, and she lazily

ambles off to reclaim her spot on my bed. She's not going to be comfortable for long if this conversation heads where I would like it to.

"If I help you with . . ." He trails off, searching for the words.

"My sex education?" I offer.

"Please don't call it that." He frowns. "It makes it sound like I'm your middle-school health teacher."

"My sexual exploration?" I try again, this time with a flirty batting of my eyelashes. I like the way he watches my lips wrap about my beer bottle as I take another swig.

"Better. Your sexual exploration. We have to make sure it won't mess with *us*."

"Mess with us how?"

"I like having you as a friend, Keaton. I don't want that to change."

I'm not sure what he means. Is this his way of saying we can't develop feelings for each other? I don't want to think that far ahead. I want to stay in this kitchen, with him, locked in place by his rich, expressive eyes.

So instead of questioning it, I just say, "Of course, Slate. Nothing could ever change between us."

"I know you wanted to find someone random to experiment with. But let's face it, those guys at the bar were lame. And I actually care about you and what you want."

"I know that." I tilt my head, studying him. "I know you care about me. I want to do this with you. You don't have to convince me."

He looks at me for a moment, clearly contemplating something. I wish I could grab him by those sexy shoulders and shake the thoughts right out of him.

"Okay," he finally says. He sets his beer down.

"Okay," I repeat, and mimic his movement.

Four Mississippi seconds of excruciating silence pass between us. Then, almost in unison, we burst into laughter.

In all our years of friendship, we've never had such a serious conversation before. Laughter feels like someone pressed the reset button, and I'm grateful for it. It's just Slate and me, and it's completely natural. It's also completely absurd, this agreement we've reached, but there's no one else I'd rather make it with.

"How the hell do we even begin?" I say, catching my breath.

"We were on the right track a minute ago."

"You know what I mean. There are definitely goals I want to reach. I have a spreadsheet—"

"I've seen your spreadsheet, Keaton," he says, "and it's very impressive. The color coding, especially."

"Okay, shut up." I chuckle.

"We'll follow it as closely as you want." He stands and takes a step toward me, and we're within touching distance again. "And maybe even improvise a bit here and there."

His mouth tilts in that lopsided smile he gets when he has an idea. It's the corniest little expression, but *damn,* I would be a liar if I said I didn't love it.

"I would like that." I place a hand on his chest, enjoying the hard muscle I feel beneath his shirt. It's like my brain is suddenly realizing he's male for the first time ever. He takes another step, and I automatically spread my legs so he can nestle himself between them.

"Good. Have I told you how much I like you in this dress?"

I'm thrown by the compliment, and even more so by the sensation of his fingers brushing back my hair. I open my mouth to say something, *anything*, but am silenced by his lips pressing against mine yet again.

My heart stutters. I gasp for a breath, but he won't let me get more than a sip of air. With his one hand cupping my jaw and the other tangling deep into my hair, I'm totally at his mercy. He angles our kiss just so, and my lips part to feel the tip of his tongue meet mine. If I thought our kiss outside was good, this one is on a whole other level.

I lean into the kiss, inviting him to give me more, to completely consume me. And consume me, he does.

His tongue sweeps against mine so expertly that I can't help but moan. His hands travel hungrily down my throat, brushing the sides of my breasts and my ribs before resting on my waist. His thumbs massage one, two deep circles against my hip bones, and I actually *buck* against him.

"Holy *shit*, Slate!" The exclamation bursts out of me. I feel like I may pass out, practically gasping for air. His breathing is just as labored, and his eyes are dark with a passion I've never seen in him. It's fucking hot.

"Let's go to your room." His voice is deeper and more seductive than anything I've ever heard. And holy hell, do I like it.

Wordlessly, I hop off the counter. Pulling him down the hall, I lead him to my bedroom. There, Slate spins me around, dragging me back into his embrace. Our kiss is messy now, our hands pulling and tugging at fabric and buttons.

Why isn't this the least bit weird? It feels so

incredibly natural to be doing this with him. It makes zero sense, but rather than question it, I kiss him back, my tongue swirling deliciously against his.

The back of my knees hit the edge of my bed a second before we both topple onto the duvet. Penny, who was most likely sleeping, squeaks in annoyance, jumping away from us in her surprise.

"Sorry, Pen," I whisper against Slate's lips, and feel his smile against my mouth. I could live off the way this man kisses.

He grinds his body against mine, one hand yanking my leg up and over his perfectly toned ass. I hook my calf there, right in the perfect dip where his lower back meets that exceptional behind. We roll to our sides, finding just the right angle where—

"Ah!" I gasp, feeling his hardness through his jeans. It presses confidently into my needy core. The silken material of my dress has long since bunched up between us, exposing the panties I wear underneath. Lacy, simple, and now entirely soaked. I wonder if he can feel my heat radiating against him. With the way his hand holds my ass and draws me even closer against him, I'm guessing yes.

We kiss for a long time until I'm breathless and almost trembling with need. Most guys would have already gotten off and left by now, but then again,

Slate's not most guys. He seems perfectly fine with just making out with me. And holy hell, his kisses are like a Class 2 narcotic—highly addictive and extremely dangerous.

His fingers dig deeply into the curve of my behind, grazing the edge of my panties with a distinct goal in mind. I open my legs for him, so his hand can slide between us. The heel of his palm presses assuredly against my clit as his fingers drag along the soaking-wet fabric covering me. I nearly come right then with the conflicting sensations of deep pressure against that bundle of nerves and the soft tickling of his long fingers gliding up and down the length of my panties.

"Slate," I whimper pleadingly.

"Is this okay?"

"Very." I whimper again.

"You want more?" he asks, meeting my eyes.

I nod without thinking. "Yeah."

He kisses my lips again and then pulls back. "How much more? I don't want to rush you. Don't want to assume . . ."

I consider his question. While part of me wants him to shut up and let me mount him like a bull at the rodeo, the other part of me appreciates that he's aware enough to set some ground rules. It's sweet, actually.

I shudder as his fingers trail over my wet panties again. "We both get to come," I say on an exhale.

"I like that idea."

"But no sex," I add.

He meets my gaze again. "Whatever you want. You're calling the shots here, Keat."

"I think we've got first base properly covered. How about we skip to third base, then?"

This seems to please him, and his mouth moves to my neck where he leaves openmouthed kisses. "As you wish."

The line is from a movie we both love—*The Princess Bride*—but my brain barely has time to catalog that before his fingers deftly push my underwear to the side, and he slides one, then two of his fingers inside me.

"*Fuck.*" His voice is a husky rumble in his throat.

My eyes sink closed as pleasure shoots through every nerve ending in my body.

I kiss him deeply while his fingers continue pumping with a fierce desire. His thumb rubs my exposed clit, and I can already feel my climax building at an astonishing rate.

Fuck, fuck, fuck. I can't let him take me there before I even see his dick!

I grasp greedily at his belt, tugging and yanking

until it comes undone. I slide my hand inside his pants, finding him so hot and hard that my body gives an involuntary clench around his fingers.

Slate makes a low sound in his throat, and I don't know if it's because he just felt that, or because he approves of my hand on his dick. Maybe both.

God, this is crazy.

I can't resist the temptation to look down between us, and when I do, I have to bite my lip from moaning at how perfect he looks. His long, veiny cock throbs against my touch, and his whole body shudders. The rhythm of his fingers sliding in and out of me doesn't falter, even as I fumble experimentally with his thick length.

"How do you . . . want me . . . to touch you?" Each word is punctuated with a small hiccuping gasp as I try to keep up with him.

His eyes are darker now with smoldering desire. "Take me by the base, firmly."

I swallow and obey, sliding my hand down. It's exciting knowing what he likes, getting to see this new side to him.

"Good. Now stroke me from the bottom to the very tip."

I do, enjoying the feel of him in my hand. He's so firm, yet his skin is so soft.

"Again. A little faster." Slate's voice is ragged, and I still can't believe it's *me* making him lose control.

I pick up my pace, a little thrill racing through me at discovering what he likes.

"Yes." When he swallows, his Adam's apple bobs, and he lets out a grunt. "Rub your thumb over—yes, right there."

I follow his orders exactly, rubbing my thumb over the wet tip of him. Stroking him while he works his long fingers inside me is better than any sex I've ever had. If just the sensations of our hands are making us this wild, what's it going to be like without the barriers of clothes? With him buried inside me? I shudder and suppress a moan.

"Perfect. Now try and match my speed," he says, challenging me with a sucking kiss on my neck.

I pick up my pace, jerking him off with zero abandon. His thumb presses onto my clit, no fumbling search necessary. He rubs quick intentional circles that fall perfectly in tempo with his long fingers pumping in and out of me.

His eyes meet mine, and our lips brush in familiarity.

"This will make you come?" I ask, my heart pounding.

"Not before you." His lips part as he watches me

in wonder.

I'm so, so close. A few more seconds and my orgasm rushes up on me like a tidal wave. The moment it hits me, I let loose a moan I never knew I had in me. My body bucks in an unrelenting dance against his hand.

"Look at me, Keat," he whispers, and I do. And with a kiss to belittle all other kisses, he falls over the edge with me.

CHAPTER
Six

Slate

THE FIRST THING I NORMALLY DO ON MONDAY mornings is catch up on all the emails that inevitably pile up over the weekend. But I'm still riding the high of my Saturday night with Keaton, and I can't stop replaying every blissful moment of discovery we shared long enough to focus.

How her delicate fingers looked wrapped around my hard cock. How she approached my instructions, tentative at first, but quickly gaining confidence. And then turning the tables on her, watching her eyes flutter and feeling her beautiful body shudder as I brought her to climax with my hands . . .

I give up on thinning out my in-box for the moment and go to the office kitchen. Maybe some coffee will help me get into the proper working groove. As I pour myself a cup, the memory of Keaton's curious, determined, lustful expression while she jerked me off strikes again, and I can't help but smile.

"What's with you?" Travis asks from where he's waiting by the microwave.

Jeez, I didn't even see him standing right there in the room. I really am distracted today.

"What do you mean?"

"Something's got you in one hell of a good mood."

I try to wipe the goofy smile off my face and shrug nonchalantly. "Just woke up on the right side of the bed, I guess. Is that a crime?" Wait, I'm acting too defensive. Way to broadcast that I've got something to hide . . . and to the resident snoop too.

"It is on a Monday morning. You get laid or what?" He smirks, and the urge to flip him off comes out of nowhere.

"You nosy or what?" I can't keep the annoyance out of my tone.

Normally it wouldn't even matter and I'd just tell him the truth—*oh yeah, I had a lucky night out recently, whatever, who cares?* But Keaton isn't some random fling I'll never see again. Even if I don't mention her name or any other details, which I never do anyway, this feels different. Something that's none of his fucking business.

Travis laughs as if he's scored a point on me. Fortunately, the microwave chooses that moment to beep, and he busies himself with the cup of oatmeal he's making. I head back to my office and close the door before he can start bugging me about my private life again.

As I mechanically answer, forward, and delete emails, my mind keeps wandering to Keaton, my best friend I just discovered a whole new side of.

The embers of attraction were always there, I've come to realize. All it took was one little kiss to blow on the ashes and make them roar to life. And now I'm unable to chase her out of my head long enough to pay any attention to work, and fighting back a boner every time I remember what we did this weekend.

Dammit, why did she have to go out of town right after I discovered just how badly I want her? How badly I've always wanted her, but somehow never realized.

My gaze strays to my phone for the billionth time, and I curse the fact that *now*, of all times, her company chose to send her to some fucking development conference for an entire week.

Screw it. I don't care if I come across as clingy; I'm not the kind of guy who plays the *who'll break down and call first?* game. And maybe taking five minutes to nail down our plans to see each other again will help me get my mind back on track.

I grab my phone and send her a message that'll hopefully put a smile on her face.

How's the conference going?

Only a few minutes pass before she answers. Either I caught her in one of the few moments she isn't busy, or she's stuck in the middle of some boring event.

Making lots of good contacts, I think. Tired, though. Looking forward to coming home.

Me too. You'll be back in town Friday night, right?

Yeah. Pretty late.

A line of bubbles wavers on the screen and I wait for her to finish responding, only for it to disappear.

Hmm. Typed something and deleted it? Well, if she won't take the plunge, I will.

So, I was wondering . . . you want to get together again next weekend?

Her reply is immediate.

> I'd like that. :) How about
> Sunday brunch?

I was expecting something more along the lines of dinner, maybe a movie, followed by spending the evening in her bed. Still, I'm hardly disappointed by the prospect of hanging out with Keaton while eating giant waffles and getting day-drunk on Bloody Marys.

> Can we do Saturday instead? Sunday
> afternoons are when I catch up
> with my mom.

It's a lame excuse. The phone call to my mom won't take more than twenty minutes of my day. I just want to see Keaton a day sooner.

> Sure. As long as I can still
> sleep in.

> As you wish. I'll come by around noon.

But I answered too soon. The second half of her

reply pops up a second after mine.

> And after, we can go back
> to my place for more
> "sexploration."

I swallow hard. It's a good thing the door is shut, and I have a desk covering my crotch right now. My coworkers don't need to see that. The only person who gets to see that is Keaton . . . five whole days from now.

God, I don't know how I'm going to make it.

♡

On my drive home from work, I detour to Keaton's apartment. Karina, Gabby, and I promised her that we'd cat-sit while she was gone, and tonight is my turn for Penny Patrol.

I unlock Keaton's door with the borrowed key and take off my shoes. When I don't immediately see Penny, I'm not concerned. I figure she'll grace me with her presence once she hears the kitty kibble rattling into her bowl.

But even after I refresh her food and water and clean her litter box, no cranky orange cat appears. Since I can't leave without even seeing her, I look underneath the couch, dining table, TV stand, even in the bathtub and behind the toilet.

Keaton's apartment isn't that big—where the fuck is she? Did she slip out the door somehow?

Finally, I check Keaton's bedroom, feeling a little weird barging in here while she's away, and spot Penny curled up like a fluffy basketball on her pillow.

"There you are. You really had me going for a minute." Penny's green eyes open ever so slightly, just the tiniest, haughty slits. I sit on the bed and stroke her rounded back. "Didn't you hear the dinner bell? What, you're too good for that stuff now?"

Ignoring my teasing, she yawns and stretches luxuriously, spreading her claws out in front of her.

Well, Penny isn't sick or missing or trapped, and she'd probably remove my hand if I tried to pick her up to take her to her food, so this is good enough for now. She'll get hungry and eat on her own, eventually. Time for me to go home.

I stand up . . . but can't help lingering, looking around, remembering what happened on this bed a mere two days ago. Just the familiar smell of Keaton is enough to simultaneously loosen my shoulders and tighten my groin.

Impatient desire hits me, and I don't even try to resist texting her.

I'm standing in your bedroom.

I blink at those words on the screen and continue typing.

I swear that's not as creepy as it sounds. I'm checking on Penny.

Keaton's reply comes a second later.

Thanks again for doing that.

Being in here . . . remembering what we did in that bed . . .

Part of me wonders if I could get Keaton to sext with me, and a smirk overtakes my mouth at the idea.

Was I that bad?

I suppress a chuckle. Leave it to Keaton to bring her trademark self-deprecating humor into a moment like this.

You know the answer to that. It's your

fault that my boxers are getting tight
remembering it.

> Don't traumatize my cat,
> Slate.

Whoops. Too late . . . I'm already
hard.

For a second, I wonder if that's totally fucking weird to send to Keaton, and I'm worried I've gone too far. But then she replies.

> There's an easy solution to
> that. Go out and get laid.

I frown at my phone. That's the last thing I want to do. Which is weird, right? But rather than over-think it, I text her back.

No thanks. I'd rather wait for you.

> Really? Then I guess I'll have
> to make it worth the wait.

Damn, woman, you're something else. I shake my

head in astonishment and pocket my phone. *All right, seriously, it's time to stop lingering here and go home.*

But as I turn to leave the bedroom, a framed picture on the back corner of Keaton's desk catches my eye. I was too preoccupied with her body to notice it the last time I was here. It's a snapshot of us with our friends from college.

I smile at how young we all look. Man, we've really changed since then. Keaton and Karina wearing matching T-shirts from their honors sorority, Gabby with that crazy rainbow-dyed hair she used to have, and . . .

My stomach sours. Tanya. Laughing and clinging to my arm like a leech.

I remember now, Tanya said I looked like an asshole in that picture. Then again, she said I was a lot of things. Stupid. Selfish. A loser only she would ever love. A disobedient animal who needed to be led around by the dick—wear this, buy me that, change majors, take some shitty job working for her father, *can't you see I'm just trying to help you?*

I grit my teeth and turn the picture frame facedown so I won't catch a glimpse of her the next time I'm here.

No, I was never the one Tanya was looking out for. She was just trying to mold me into the impossible fantasy she carried around in her mind. The perfect arm-candy breadwinner who would never, ever embarrass or inconvenience her by acting like an independent human being. And when I couldn't be that mind-reading robot who always did and said and looked exactly how she wanted, she finally lost patience and kicked me to the curb.

Looking back on it now, I can tell what a huge bullet I dodged. But at the time, I was wrapped hopelessly around her finger, and her rejection ripped my heart out. Just goes to show how stupid love makes you, I guess.

Well, it royally sucked for a while, but I picked up the pieces and learned my lesson—relationships just aren't worth the hassle. I've had enough of that pain and stress to last the rest of my life. Tanya was my first serious girlfriend, and I resolved long ago that she'd be my last. I have better things to pour my emotional energy into. Like a best friend who actually gives a flying fuck about me.

The pressure of a paw pulls me out of my bad memories. Penny has stepped on my toes with her full twenty-pound weight, and is looking sternly up at me.

Reaching down to scratch her fuzzy forehead, I let out a deep sigh. "I can't wait for Keaton to come back either."

CHAPTER
Seven

Keaton

I CRINGE AS SLATE DUMPS THE CONTENTS OF YET another sugar packet into his coffee.

"Explain something to me," I say, speaking mid-chew through my breakfast burrito bursting with chorizo, cheese, and salsa.

It's been a week since I've seen him, so a reunion at our favorite brunch spot was the most natural plan. Our food has just arrived, and Slate is fixing his coffee the way he likes it—one third coffee, one third milk, one third sugar packets. I think we're on raw sugar number six now?

"How have you not died yet from a sugar overdose with how you take your coffee?"

"I like what I like, and my body respects that. We're totally in sync." He places a hand on his chest. My gaze lingers on the way his large hand looks pressed in earnest against his heart.

"How nice for you and your body," I say with a mock sneer, taking an obnoxious bite out of my burrito. Damn, this is so good.

If this were a date, I would have ordered something simple and cute, like a neat stack of buttermilk pancakes, or two eggs over easy. Fork and knife, with little chance of spilling anything down the front of my shirt. But this is no date, and Slate knows exactly what I like for brunch.

We'd barely sat down when he asked our waiter for one sunrise burrito and a black coffee for me, followed by his own order of a classic Denver omelet with extra bacon on the side. I don't have to worry about salsa dribbling off my chin around Slate, just like he doesn't have to worry about me judging his coffee preferences.

Well, I still tease. I've missed him, after all.

"Tell me about the trip," he says.

"Same old."

I sigh, recalling to him the endless seminars and dry business dinners. Business trips start to bleed together when you've been in the same job for as many years as I have. This time, however, I'm excited to share an update with Slate on my own personal research.

"You wouldn't believe how thin the walls of our

hotel were." I lean in, lowering my voice in the small diner. I'm very aware of the proximity of other unassuming customers. "The couple in the neighboring room was having the most vocal and elaborate sex I've ever heard."

I then proceed to recount the night to Slate—the volume of the moaning, the colorful language shared between the couple, the frankly alarming banging of the headboard against the wall.

"I think they were role-playing 'sheriff and prostitute.' It was absolutely fascinating."

Slate gives me a skeptical look.

"What?"

"I have this image of you with your ear to the wall, scribbling notes onto a notepad to transcribe later into your spreadsheet."

I hold my finger up in a "hold on" gesture as I dig through my purse. I pull out my planner, where I keep all my notes, as well as an abridged schedule of my Sexploration Goals.

"You took notes." He nods, as if this was entirely expected.

"Of course I did. This is great material." I wave the page in front of him until he swipes it out of my hand.

"'Ride me. Break me like the naughty wild horse I

am.' Oh my God. This isn't even good dirty talk." He shakes his head in disgust.

"It isn't?" I frown.

"I shouldn't say that. If it works for them, then it's good."

"How do you determine what's good dirty talk and what isn't?" I click my pen, ready to write down every piece of wisdom he has to offer.

Slate shrugs, looking as casual as ever, even about such a heated and intense topic. It's amazing how comfortable he is with sex—it's also why he's the perfect teacher for me.

"It's trial and error. Starting with the basic territory. How it feels, things you'd like to do to your partner. If you want to get into this kind of thing," he taps on the edge of my notebook with his fork, "then you have to find some common ground."

"Other than sex?"

"Yes. If you want to role-play or start simple with metaphors, it should revolve around something you both love. Something that turns you both on."

"So, what turns you on?"

Slate isn't at all fazed by my point-blank question. "Ah, that's too simple. It has to be something that makes both of us horny. For instance," he picks up a strip of bacon, "brunch."

I nearly choke on my coffee. "Brunch does *not* make me horny."

"Really?" He lifts the bacon to his mouth, barely grazing the edge across his lower lip.

My gaze is glued to his mouth, following the shiny drop of bacon grease it leaves there. He opens his mouth and places the bacon on his tongue, closing his eyes to fully appreciate the taste of salty sweetness.

As his eyes flutter closed, I feel the telltale shiver of sexual excitement creep down the nape of my neck to my tailbone. The look on his face makes me wonder what he'd look like, verging on the edge of orgasm, with my mouth around his cock.

Whoa. Where did that thought come from?

His eyes flash open, dark and dilated, and he digs his teeth into the juicy slab of bacon. He holds the other half up to me, hovering temptingly before my lips. I lean forward and take a nibble.

"Okay," I say, "you've proven your point. That was hot."

"So, talk brunch to me," he says, grinning through another bite of bacon.

As if on cue, an adorably cute elderly couple sit right behind Slate in the neighboring booth. I widen my eyes and nod my head in their direction.

Slate peeks over his shoulder, turns back to me, and shrugs.

I roll my eyes. *Okay, Keaton, you've got this. If you can talk dirty in a quiet, family-owned diner, you can talk dirty anywhere.*

"Speaking of spice, this burrito is hotter than usual . . ." I trail off, using a finger to stir the complimentary ice water that came with my meal.

Slate eyes my finger, amused as to where this is going.

"I like it hot, you know," I say, drawing a lazy circle around the rim of the glass.

Slate shakes his head. "You've got to sell me, Keat."

Leaning in closer, I blink slowly, batting my eyelashes at him, and my voice drops low. "I want to swallow your smoothie, Slate."

I lift his fruity drink to my lips and take a sip, catching one of the strawberries with my tongue. Drawing my finger into my mouth with a slow suck, I begin moving the berry around in my mouth, occasionally flashing my tongue.

Slate watches me, his eyes never leaving the wet glimmer of my lips.

At first, I feel stupid, like this is never going to work, but then I see his expression—the way his eyes are half-lidded and focused on my mouth, and I feel emboldened.

I moan softly. "Mmm, I love having it in my mouth."

Finally, I swallow. My finger, still wet, runs a lazy line down my neck to my collarbone. He follows my every movement, just like I want.

"Is it warm in here?" I ask playfully.

Slate chuckles, shaking his head in disbelief. "Okay, fine, you pass, you're amazing. Now let's get out of here."

As we get up, I notice the elderly couple staring almost too intently at their menus.

At the counter, Slate pays for both of our meals. I choose not to give him grief about it this time, because I'd rather take our lesson back to my apartment as quickly as possible rather than prolong it with a gender-equality debate.

I'm eyeing the pastries as he swipes his card at the register. "Do you want anything else before we leave? The muffins look extra fresh today. My treat."

Slate considers the offer for a moment, perusing the glass case briefly before he decides. "Not right now. Thank you, though."

We turn toward the door, his hand resting casually on the small of my back.

"That's okay," I murmur into his ear. "You can munch on my muffin anytime."

Slate stops dead in his tracks, his breath caught in his throat.

"What?" I laugh. "Too much for you?"

"You're killing me." He shakes his head, but his laughter fills me up with joy.

"Next time we come, I could butter your bagel."

His hand gently covers my mouth and he plants a kiss against my cheek. My face heats up immediately at the intimacy of the gesture.

"Please, for the love of God, stop. You've passed. With flying colors."

I grin. Slate is still chuckling as we begin the short walk back to my apartment.

That's the greatest compliment I could have asked for.

♡

My first impulse upon entering the apartment is to check off *dirty talk* on my spreadsheet. I like a job well done, and I like a solid checkmark even more. However, Slate takes me by the waist, twists me around, and pulls me away from the table.

"What? I passed!"

"Follow-up assessment. Gotta make sure it stuck."

With a kiss against my neck, he guides me to the couch and positions me so that he's on top, fully in command. Soon, we're lip-locked and my legs are wrapped tightly around his hips. Slate's kisses are deep and insistent. I sense a passion that's been brewing ever since I teased him with that strawberry. *Note to self: that trick does wonders.*

I break away from his lips. "How am I supposed to talk dirty to you if I don't have access to oxygen?"

"Point taken."

He begins unbuttoning the casual flannel shirt I'm wearing and plants small kisses down my breastbone. Holding himself over me with one strong arm, he deftly pops open each of my buttons his free hand. His fingers brush his lightly over my newly exposed skin before his lips follow, leaving soft, nibbling kisses in their wake.

I'm trying to stay focused, but *goddamn* is it hard with Slate's tongue dipping into my belly button like that.

"You liked that muffin bit, didn't you?" I murmur, hinting at my hopes for his destination.

"I did like it," he whispers against my hip bone. My pants are unbuckled, unzipped, and pushed down over my behind at the command of his strong hands.

"How much did you like it?" I ask, dragging my fingers through his tousled hair.

He digs his teeth into my hip bone, teasing the sensitive skin there, and I stifle a gasp. One of my arms flies up over my head to grasp for leverage on the armrest.

"I've been thinking about your muffin ever since."

My pants are off, my lacy underwear exposed. Slate nuzzles his nose against the fabric. I can feel his hot breath dance against my still-clothed clit.

"Mmm," is all I can manage as I squirm against him, desperate for him to just get on with it and put those unholy lips against my—

I buck against his mouth as he presses his lips there. I want to tear off my underwear.

"Please," I beg. "Please, I'll do anything."

"Anything? That's awfully tempting."

Slate looks up at me with a smirk that drips with sex. Then he grasps my ass with the hands of a man who knows exactly what he wants, and drags me closer. With two fingers, he pulls aside the stretchy fabric and stares down at me.

"Damn." His voice is husky, his tone almost reverent.

I can feel how soaking wet I am, even before he drags his thumb from my opening to my clit in a splendid figure eight.

"What do you want?"

"I want," I gasp out, trying to catch my breath, "you to lick me."

"Where?"

I could clamp his head between my thighs and push his lips against me if I wanted to. And *hot damn,* do I want to. But I know this is a test, and he wants me to say it. I love how confident and bold he is, how sexy. It makes me want to try . . .

"I want you to," I say, my voice low, "lick my clit."

His tongue presses against my clit in immediate obedience. My spine curves in an involuntary effort to give him the perfect angle. His tongue laps, swirls, and dances against my most intimate flesh.

"Oh yes. *Shit!*" My voice is loud. Maybe too loud. Do I care? Not at all.

Spreading my knees wider, I lift my hips into his wild kisses. His finger pushes inside me, pumping in perfect tempo with each suck and lick. Who knew that smartass mouth could be so skilled at pleasuring a woman?

He moans against me, and the low vibration of his voice floods through my body. I feel the edge rushing up on me again, and welcome it with a cry of pure satisfaction. He doesn't stop, doesn't let up at all as I suddenly come so hard, and for so long, I'm left light-headed.

Slate helps me ride through the quakes, pressing his lips against my inner thighs as I shake softly from the experience. When my body is finally in my control again, I sink into the couch, completely sated.

He lifts his head from between my legs. "Hey," he says casually.

"Hi." I laugh. "I didn't know you were so good at that."

He smiles almost bashfully before his usual confident smirk takes over. I can tell he likes the compliment. Even more so, he likes hearing it from me.

"I only give my best to the best." He draws himself up into a seated position on the couch.

"I'll have to return the favor then," I say, lowering myself to the floor so that I'm kneeling before him. For a second, I think he might stop me, but then as my hands find his thighs and rub up and down the denim fabric, familiarizing myself with the feel of his sinewy muscles, his eyes darken with desire.

"How do you plan on doing that?" he asks, leaning back against the couch, giving me all the access I need to unclasp his belt.

I undo that barrier with quick and confident fingers, letting the buckle of his belt fall against the couch.

"Well," I say, my eyes never leaving his, "I plan to suck on your huge cock."

Here goes nothing.

CHAPTER Eight

Slate

I SHIFT TO SIT ON THE EDGE OF THE COUCH WITH my knees parted. With her deep blue eyes locked on mine, Keaton kneels between my thighs.

My heart starts to hammer in anticipation. I was fine with waiting my turn—more than fine, because it meant I got the chance to pleasure her, to feel her quake apart under my tongue—but now I'm so ready, it physically hurts.

Carefully, like she's dealing with a live nuclear missile instead of a dick, Keaton slides her hand under the band of my boxer briefs and takes out my cock.

"Should I put my mouth on it?" she asks.

I place my hand on her cheek and stroke my thumb over her skin. God, she's so fucking adorable. "First, you don't have to do this. You don't have to do anything you don't want."

"I know that." Her lips turn up in a slight smile.

"Good. Second, you never have to ask. The answer is always going to be yes . . . yes, you can put your mouth on it."

Keaton smiles and rolls her eyes. But rather than lean in closer like I'm expecting, she blinks up at me. "Slate?"

"Yeah?"

"After this . . . I mean, after my whole list is done, we'll go back to being just friends, right?"

"Of course." I wouldn't have it any other way. The only reason I agreed to this whole thing was because I knew we'd never let this come between us. Our friendship is rock solid.

"Good," she says, and her mouth is so close to my cock, I can feel the heat of her breath.

Fuck.

I want to feel her mouth there so badly. If this were anyone else, I'd place my hand on the back of her neck and guide her down. But this is Keaton, and this is about her, so instead I wait patiently.

Tentatively, her lips slide over the head of my cock, and I suck in a sharp breath. Just that hot, wet touch feels amazing all on its own, to say nothing of the incredible view.

Fuck, I'm so hard for her, which is crazy. This is

Keaton. My buddy. My pal. The friend I share a pizza and a six-pack with on weekends while watching raunchy R-rated comedies.

And now she's on her knees in front me, treating my dick to slow, wet kisses that are about to make me lose my damn mind.

Shit. It won't take much to make me explode.

A little unsteadily, I continue my instructions. "That feels nice. I want you to stroke it up and down, following your mouth with your hand . . ."

I watch her stroke what she can't fit into her mouth, still sucking on the head of my cock like it's a Popsicle.

Fuck.

"And that's the basic idea." My voice comes out too hoarse, and I clear my throat.

Then Keaton dives down with a vengeance. The head of my cock hits the back of her throat and two things happen at once—my hips jerk, and she recoils with a cough.

"Shit." I fight to regain control. "Slow down. It's not a deep-throating race."

She withdraws slightly to mutter, "Whoops. Sorry."

"No need to apologize. I just feel bad you gagged yourself."

I stroke her cheek with my thumb. Truth be told, it felt pretty great on my end, but she can't keep that up.

"Don't bite off more than you can chew." At her deadpan glare, I add, "Sorry, poor choice of words. What I meant was, don't push yourself so hard you're not having a good time anymore. It makes it better all the way around when I know the woman is enjoying herself too."

Telling the world's most hard-driving woman to be less ambitious . . . yeah, we'll see how that goes.

She looks at my cock with a slight frown, then takes another stab at it, this time using her mouth only on the upper third and letting her hand take care of the rest.

"There you go," I say, my voice gruff. Once she seems to have the basic idea down, I add, "Try moving your tongue a little."

She makes a noise of acknowledgment. I shiver at the brief vibration, then again, more deeply, at the gentle writhing against the sensitive underside of my cock. But the slow, steady rhythm is just enough to get me near the edge without pushing me over.

"Faster." My voice comes out husky with need.

Her tongue shifts gears to a rapid, feathery flicking like what I used on her clit earlier. That speed feels better, but now there's not quite enough contact to satisfy me.

"Ah . . ."

I'm trying my best to impart some wisdom here, but Keaton's adorably amateur attempts at blowing me make it hard to stay coherent. Just like in our first encounter, she's tiptoeing around my dick like she's defusing a bomb. It's hilarious, but also fucking sexy, because it's just so *Keaton*. Nobody else would approach sex quite so analytically. She's hot even when she doesn't mean to be. And her technique certainly isn't *bad* . . . but she needs a little guidance.

"Hang on." I place my hand on her cheek to halt her. I'm not just a dude getting his dick sucked. I'm a friend trying to teach. And as good as it feels, I know she can do better.

She pulls off with a faint, wet pop and looks up at me, her brow furrowed with confusion and more than a little impatience. "What's wrong? Am I that bad?"

"No, not at all, but I can tell you're thinking too much." My lips quirk. "As usual."

She lets go of me completely to sit back on her heels. "Thinking is bad? Then what should I do, just slap it around randomly?"

"What I mean is, just try to relax. It's just a dong,

not a supercomputer." I grin when she cracks up. "There you go. Laughing is a good start. Sex is supposed to be about having fun."

Still chuckling, she gives me a skeptical, raised-eyebrow smirk. "Laugh at a man's penis. Hang on, let me write that hot tip down."

"Not *at* him, *with* him. You know what I'm trying to say . . . don't take things too seriously. You have to go with the flow and just do what feels right."

"That's what I was trying to do—plan out what would feel good for you." Her lips purse in frustration.

Maybe we need a different angle of attack. I rub my chin, figuring out what will make the most sense to her. "How about this? Forget everything you've ever read or heard about what men like in bed and just rely on my feedback. Every man is different, anyway, so reading his reactions works better than trying to memorize a bunch of stuff like you're studying for a test."

"So, playing a sexy version of that game Hot and Cold?" she asks.

"Sort of. Just do whatever comes into your head, and if I like it, I'll let you know."

She nods slowly. "I think I can handle that."

I tweak her nose. "No thinking, remember?"

"Yeah, yeah." Resting her elbows on my thighs, she puts one hand around my cock, letting the fingertips of her other hand rest on my leg, then lowers her mouth back down.

I let out a moan of pleasure to encourage her. "Mmm . . . much better."

She seems to be using her hands and tongue smoothly now, so I decide to move the lesson forward a little more. "Yes. Fuck. Now, cup my balls. Rub them with your palm, gently."

She obeys, and I don't have to try to remember to moan. I couldn't hold back, even if I wanted to. My eyes practically roll to the back of my head. *I knew things would go a lot smoother once she got out of her own head.*

I fight through the growing haze of pleasure to keep guiding her, reassuring her constantly that she's doing great, stroking her hair and neck and jawline and whatever other silky skin I can reach. She responds well to my filthy praise, her movements becoming less calculated and more sensual, even letting out the occasional dreamy murmur.

She's getting off on this, I realize with a jolt of heat. That's what made the difference. Turning her on got her into the zone.

I love watching her take me. Her eyes are closed,

her long lashes resting against high cheekbones, and the delicate column of her throat works me up and down.

"Just like that."

I place one hand on her head and pump my hips up toward her mouth. She makes a murmured noise of pride, clearly enjoying the fact that my control is slipping.

"*Fuck.*"

I roll my hips up and she takes the cue, intensifying the strokes of her tongue and hand. I won't last much longer; it feels like I've been ready and waiting all day. My balls start drawing up tight against my body.

"Ah, Keaton . . ." I groan. "Gonna come soon . . . not sure if you want me to . . ."

She doesn't stop, doesn't let up at all as I pull a deep breath into my lungs, fighting to maintain control. She knows how this works, right? Surely, she doesn't want . . . I mean, I can't come in her mouth . . .

"*Keat* . . ." I growl. "If you don't wanna taste it, now's the time to—"

Instead of pulling away, she speeds up, and I choke on my words. My muscles tighten, bliss washes through me, and my cock pulses right into her warm, waiting mouth. She keeps working me through it until I gasp for her to stop, so hypersensitive that I can't take any more.

At first, I think she's going to spit it out. But then a determined look appears on her face, like this is a game she's playing to win. Giving me a long-lashed, sultry glance, she swallows audibly.

I gulp right back. *Holy fuck, that's one of the hottest things I've ever seen.*

My fingers still tangled in her long, dark hair, I lean down to crush our lips together, tasting the bitter traces of my own release. She moans throatily into my mouth and responds with unashamed hunger, all nipping teeth and lashing tongue.

We indulge in the smoldering kiss for a good long while before she pulls back to ask, low and breathy, "How was that?"

If she wants a little ego-stroking, no problem— she's more than earned it. "Fucking amazing," I answer truthfully.

I help her up onto the couch, and we settle back against the cushions.

"So, did you enjoy yourself too?" I ask, tugging up my boxers.

She tilts her head. "Wasn't this about you?"

"I mean, sure, you gave me an orgasm—a fucking

incredible one, just so you know—but I still want to hear if you got something out of it. You shouldn't blow a guy just because you feel like you have to."

She makes a thoughtful noise. "You know . . . yeah, I did like it." A playful, open smile curves her lips. "You were right about not thinking. When I focused on making you feel good, I got into this headspace where I just intuitively knew what to do."

"Glad I could help," I reply. "Just so you know, you didn't have to swallow that."

She grins. "I know."

Then she leans on me, and without even thinking about it, I loop my arm around her soft, bare shoulders. Her sex-tousled hair rests against my cheek. I inhale the scents of sweat and pleasure and something uniquely Keaton, and a quiet sigh of contentment escapes her.

Everything feels so damn good right now. It must just be the sex hormones, though.

Then Keaton's phone chimes from her purse across the room. She stretches with an adorable little squeak and mutters, "Shit. I've got to get going." Do I imagine the note of reluctance in her voice?

I frown. "Why?"

"Karina and Gabby and I have plans to see *Mommy Troubles* today, and I totally lost track of time. That was my alarm telling me I have half an hour to get to the theater. Mind if I abandon you so I can shower real quick?"

Despite my disappointment, I smirk. Guess she worked up a sweat. "Go right ahead. It's your place." Hell, she could easily kick me out with the excuse of needing to get ready. But maybe, some part of me hopes she wants me to stick around as badly as I want to stay.

In ten minutes, she emerges dressed in a short, silky robe with a small towel twisted around her hair, and I openly admire her body, damp and flushed from the hot water. I liked how she smelled before, all musky from sex, but I also like how she smells now, all clean and flowery-sweet with the feminine perfumes of her shampoo and soap.

Raising one eyebrow in mock indignation, she plants her hands on her rounded hips, pushing out her chest. "You checking me out?"

"Of course. Why wouldn't I?"

She gives me a giggle and a little bump with her hip as she walks past me back into the bedroom. She pulls some clothes out of her closet and starts pulling them on while I lounge on her bed.

"Sorry to chase you off so early."

"No worries." Leaning back against the

headboard, I watch the delectable body I just had the privilege of pleasuring gradually disappear under fabric.

"Are you going to tell the girls you just completed a successful blow job?"

She shoots me a weird look. "Why would I do that?"

"That's how all this started, wasn't it? At Karina's vegetable-themed bachelorette party." I raise my hand to mime sliding a long, thick object in and out of my mouth.

She lets out a snort of laughter and shakes her head. "No, I think I'll keep this private. This is nobody's business but ours."

"Good point," I say with a nod. "I don't kiss and tell either."

And I really do agree. But for some reason, I feel a little . . . ambivalent about this. On one hand, not only does it make sense to avoid spreading gossip, it's somehow gratifying to be privy to Keaton's secrets—to see a side of her that nobody else gets to know about.

On the other, I can't help wondering exactly why she's keeping this under wraps. Is she ashamed of fucking around with me? Maybe she just feels awkward about the fact that she needs sex lessons at all and doesn't want to risk any teasing about her lack of experience. Gabby especially has a bad habit of taking jokes too far sometimes.

But still . . .

I shake my head. This train of thought is going nowhere. Keaton and I are going back to being just friends once her sex to-do list is complete, so it makes sense why she wouldn't want to tell anyone. Right?

I try to turn off my brain and just enjoy my last glimpses of her body. They'll have to sustain me until we meet again.

After she finishes dressing, she walks me to the front door, where I hesitate with my hand on the knob.

"Hey, um . . ." I feel like I should do more than just say good-bye, since we just spent such a mind-blowing day together. But I have no idea what.

Kissing outside the bedroom feels too romantic, so I probably shouldn't kiss her, even though I really want to. Shaking hands would be ridiculous—we're not at a freaking business meeting. Maybe a nice, casual, totally friends-but-not-more-than-friends high five?

"Yeah?" Keaton prompts me.

Finally, I settle on holding out my closed fist.

"Thanks for today. It was . . . really fun."

She laughs and fist-bumps me. "I had fun too. But I'm the one who should be thanking you for teaching me. Let's do it again soon."

I return her playful grin. "Hell yeah. Text me when you're done, and we can make plans." As I start down the hall to the elevator, I add, "Enjoy your chick flick."

Totally straight-faced, she sticks out her tongue at me.

I laugh, tucking my hands in my pockets, and walk away, already looking forward to our next time.

CHAPTER
Nine

Keaton

"THIS MAN IS LIKE A DRUG," THE ACTRESS says on the big screen. "He's more than a one-hit wonder. He's an addiction."

I cough noisily into my cocktail napkin, stifling a laugh.

Karina, sitting to my left, turns to me with a look of concern. "Are you okay?" she whispers, trying to keep her voice down in the posh movie theater we've chosen for our girls' night out.

Gabby, Karina, and I used to have movie nights when we lived together in college. Back then, it was on a futon, snuggled up with fleece blankets and individual bottles of wine. Now, we try to class it up by heading to theaters like this one with big comfy seats, surround sound, and expensive snacks.

We may have exchanged our bowls of potato chips for made-to-order sushi, but the foundation remains the same. My best friends, some guilty-pleasure food, and a terrible movie.

"This movie is just so good," I deadpan as best as I can through my giggles.

"Shh!" Gabby shushes us from where she's seated on the other side of Karina. The bride-to-be is nestled between Gabby and me on this luxurious love seat, complete with an electric ice bucket to keep our wine chilled.

It's safe to say that Karina is sandwiched between two very different viewing experiences.

Gabby wipes her eyes with tissues, emotionally taken by this masterpiece of romance. She's been a huge sucker for romantic movies for as long as I've known her. Yes, romantic movies highlighting *monogamous* love. Who knew the queen of hookups could be such a softie?

While Gabby wipes her eyes, I dab at my blouse with a napkin, trying to recover from when I dribbled my cocktail down my front in mid-laugh. Somewhere along the line since my college days, I lost the ability to take these romantic movies seriously. They're just so unrealistic.

Karina reads my mind, as usual. "It is kind of over the top," she says, sucking on the straw of her fruity cocktail.

"Right? Maybe I'm nitpicking, but if what's-her-face is actually a journalist for the *New Yorker*, why is she using mixed metaphors? One-hit wonder is a music term. Addiction is . . . drugs," I whisper back, and Karina laughs.

Gabby leans over the bride-to-be to better scrutinize me. "You're just jealous she's gonna end up with Mr. Tall, Dark, and Handsome."

"Tall, dark, handsome, and emotionally unavailable. He's a total playboy! So he's pretty," I counter, rolling my eyes.

"Gimme some of that attraction any day of the week!" Gabby lifts her drink in a toast, and she and Karina clink glasses in alliance.

Fine, let them have their romance.

An emotional montage begins on the screen. The actress is embarrassingly lost without her man. She pines at her window. She pines in an elevator. She pines at her desk. She's finally outside! Oh no, she's pining on a park bench.

We've all seen this scene before in about ten other movies. So we turn to each other to continue the conversation, much to the dismay of the viewers behind us.

"I can't get Toby to commit to come with me to the wedding," Gabby complains, rolling her eyes. "So

I'm thinking that I'm just going to ditch him and ask Sammie."

"Is that the tennis guy?" Karina asks.

"No, that's Ben. Sammie is the sexy bartender lady who gives me free drinks. We have an arrangement," she says with a wink. Gabby is truly extraordinary.

"Won't that piss Toby off?" I ask, always impressed with how well Gabby juggles so many sexual partners at once.

"He had his chance. He won't step it up for one of the most important days of my life. I'm seeing this beauty married off to a truly wonderful man." She grasps Karina's hand, who smiles broadly at the compliment. "But his response was that he doesn't know what 'July has in store for him yet.'"

"Ugh." Karina sighs. "That is such a red flag. If I narrowed it down, that's probably the number one reason I'm marrying Mateo. He has a physical day planner that he *actually uses*. And an address book!"

"That's hot," I say with complete honesty.

"That's what I'm saying! He's got the whole week before the wedding marked up with preparation planning." Karina grins.

Gabby and I exchange secret smiles. It makes both of us so happy to see Karina like this in the weeks before her big day—excited, glowing, and feeling cherished.

"Speaking of Tennis Ben," Gabby says. "Keat, do you want me to set you up? He could be your plus-one."

"I'm good, actually." I laugh.

"Come on," Karina begs. "Please bring a plus-one. You know I would dance with you the whole night, but then Mateo's parents might talk . . ."

"Seriously, I'm good in the plus-one department."

There's an obvious beat of silence as Karina eyes me. "Wait, are you saying you're bringing a plus-one to the wedding?"

"Has this ever happened?" Gabby asks, and she and Karina spend a little too much time analyzing this. They converse with each other, locking me out of the conversation.

"No, I don't think so."

"Not even—"

"No, this is truly monumental."

"Okay," I say, jumping in, "I don't have anyone specific in mind yet, but I want to bring somebody. So I'm looking at my options."

Gabby and Karina exchange another look.

"So you're going to ask Slate," Gabby says, rolling

her eyes like he doesn't count.

"N-no. There's a really hot guy at work who I get along with."

They both look at me, the skepticism in their eyes like a microphone thrust toward my face. I take the bait, jumping to my defense. There actually *is* a guy at work. His name is Jerome.

"He's in his mid-thirties, and by some blessing of the universe, still single. He's a marketing coordinator from the Toronto branch, so not only is he smart, he's also foreign."

"Is Toronto even foreign?" Gabby asks.

I steamroll past that question. "He used to run track back when he was a teenager, and he misses it, so now he runs marathons for charity. Like he literally sweats for a good cause."

Gabby and Karina are only mildly impressed by all this.

I can't fathom how they don't agree that Jerome is perfect. He's pretty much every one of my plus-one goals. It would be a dream to have this kind of arm candy at my best friend's wedding. Candy that is both delicious to look at and delicious to fantasize about.

Besides, we aren't committed to each other, so if I'm not feeling it, I can easily keep him focused on making the most of the open bar and buffet while I spend the night dancing with my girlfriends. Or, at the end of the night, I can test out all that I've been working on with Slate. No harm, no foul. Just the New and Improved Keaton, diving in headfirst!

"Jerome sounds nice." Karina smiles, but I can tell her heart isn't in it.

"What?" *What could possibly be the problem here?*

"I just thought you were going to bring Slate," she says, and Gabby nods in agreement.

"Why would I bring Slate?" I hear myself asking, my voice coming out too high-pitched. I instantly regret asking them the question. My throat goes dry.

"Uh," Karina says, "maybe it's because he's a ton of fun and clearly cares about you."

"Yeah." Gabby shrugs. "I mean, Jerome feels like a pit stop to the main destination."

"Jerome is not a pit stop." I frown. *Is he?*

And Slate can't be the destination. For one, Slate has zero interest in being anyone's destination. I know that very well. Tanya did a freaking number on him, and he swore off relationships ever since. He has way too much fun playing the field to ever change.

Karina takes another sip, then says, "Kinda feels

that way."

We all turn back to the screen. Now the two protagonists are mashing their faces together in a climactic scene of passion. With the orchestral swell and the dramatic rainfall, everything about this scene feels contrived. I struggle not to roll my eyes.

I sink deeper into the love seat, supremely annoyed.

Jerome *is* a real person. True, I would have never considered asking him out until now. He's the kind of guy you ogle from afar until you watch him slide right through your fingers because you never had the guts to take that step.

It's in this moment that I realize my sexploration has been about more than improving my blow-job skills, or sharpening my dirty-talk routine. It's about amping up my confidence to what I can bring to a relationship. And when I'm ready, I'll be that much more prepared. Maybe to ask out Jerome, or maybe someone else. My own personal sex coach will turn me into a certified love machine.

Watching this two-dimensional potato of a woman fall for yet another heart-of-gold playboy, it becomes very clear to me that I am not her, and certainly will never be. The actress spent most of this movie pining for a man who only showed her affection in brief, confusing encounters. And then suddenly, there's a big moment when he admits he can't stay away from her any longer. What? I want to puke. Why is this so dramatic?

I'm suddenly even more grateful for my friendship with Slate. We've had such a positive partnership this past week. Good conversations, good laughs, good sexy times. No drama whatsoever.

A quiet thought pops into in my head. *He's the healthiest relationship you could ask for.* The difference? I would *never* pine for Slate. He's a friend, and only a friend. Don't they always say not to date your friends? Sure, he has a top-notch sense of humor. And he's a great conversationalist. And he gets along bizarrely well with Penny. And his ass is absolutely—

No. Stop, Keaton.

Slate is not boyfriend material. He's not looking for a girlfriend; he's the king of hookups. Thinking it could lead to something more would make me no better than this dumb-as-a-box-of-rocks heroine in the movie. And I'm much too smart for that nonsense.

Before my mind travels too far out of Rational Town, I redirect my attention back to Karina and

Gabby. *Focus, Keaton. It's girls' night.*

As I stare blankly at the movie screen, I repeat over and over in my mind. *I will not get in over my head with Slate. I will not get in over my head with Slate. I will not get in over my head with Slate . . .*

CHAPTER
Ten

Slate

THIS IS IT. TONIGHT'S THE BIG NIGHT.

After practicing for so long with manual and oral and dirty talk, giving me just enough of Keaton to whet my appetite for more, we've arrived at the main event. I'm finally going to discover what it feels like to be inside her.

My blood has been humming with eagerness all day. As soon as I hit SEND on my last work email, I text Keaton.

When will you be done?

> I'm just wrapping up now, actually. Impatient for tonight? :P

My lips quirk. Yes, I'm always impatient to touch

Keaton, but that's beside the point.

I want to take you out to dinner.

A long pause, then one lone word of reply.

Why?

I ponder her question for a minute. Honestly, I don't have a solid answer. But what does it matter why I want to? Treating her to a nice evening just seems like the right thing to do. Tonight will be an important first for us, so I feel like I should give the proceedings some . . . romance is the wrong word. A little more ceremony than usual? Whatever you'd call it, I want to do more than just meet up at my place to screw. Some acknowledgment that tonight is special.

Finally, I type back with the safest response I can think of.

We have to eat sometime,
don't we?

I can just grab something
quick on my own.

True, but I was thinking a nice meal.
We'll need our energy for all the
exercise we're going to get later.

                              Oh, really?

I can perfectly imagine her tone, skepticism turning to playful interest. And then my phone chimes
with her reply.

                Well, if you insist . . . then
                  sure, dinner sounds fun. I'm
                            ready when you are.

On my way. See you in 15.

When I arrive, Keaton's waiting for me outside
her building's front entrance. In her black dress pants
and white collared blouse, she exudes a smart, classy
professionalism that makes me imagine her closing
big deals, gracefully fielding tough calls with intimi-
dating bigwigs, the almighty queen of her office—as
well as all the not-safe-for-work things we could do
in that office with the door locked. Of course, she'd
look hot in anything, but each outfit she wears is a
different kind of sexy, and I appreciate seeing every

possible variation.

I park in the closest open space and get out to open the passenger door for her.

Walking over, she says, "You didn't have to do that," even as she fights a smile.

"I know," I reply simply.

She shakes her head at me, still smiling, and climbs into the passenger seat. I shut the door and walk around the car to get back in the driver's seat.

"So, where are we going?" she asks, buckling herself in.

I flash her a mischievous smirk. "It's a surprise."

While browsing online yesterday, I came across a new Italian bistro I thought she might like. The reviews said it was quiet and intimate, had a sizable wine list, and offered attentive service. Overall, it sounded like a good date place, and I made the snap decision to try it out. As delicious as the cheap, greasy burritos at our usual place can be, trying something more upscale will be refreshing. Plus, the chance to treat Keaton makes me smile. We never do things like this together, and it seems only right that we should—especially since she's treating me to something very precious later.

We slip into easy conversation, swapping stories about our day. And when we arrive, I usher Keaton inside with my hand on the small of her back. It's hard to miss the way her lips quirk up in a smile.

The restaurant is cozy and unpretentious—warm, with soft lighting, plain brick walls, hardwood floors, no more than a dozen tables draped with white cloths. The hostess seats us at a table where we can see over a half wall and into the bustling kitchen.

Keaton scans the menu for a minute before her blue eyes turn huge. "Oh my God. They have lobster macaroni and cheese? I didn't even know that was a thing." She sneaks an uncertain glance at me over the top of her menu.

I shrug with a smile. "If you want it, go for it." *My philosophy on life.*

She bites her lip and grins. "I mean, I practically have to. This opportunity doesn't present itself every day."

How is she so fucking cute? That face would be worth the price of any dish.

When the waiter returns, I order the lobster mac for her, along with veal ravioli for me and whatever wine the sommelier recommends. He brings over a bottle of Chablis and pours us each a glass.

I sip slowly, enjoying the earthy, tart flavor. "Was this a nice surprise?"

"It's wonderful." With a sultry glint in her eyes,

Keaton adds, "But I'm more excited about what you've got up your sleeve for later tonight."

My mind goes blank. X-rated thoughts have filtered through my brain all day while at work, but now's not the time to discuss them. I'll end up sporting a hard-on all through dinner.

I take a deep breath to clear my head. "No spoilers. You'll just have to wait and see."

"The surprises don't end with dinner?" Her grin spreads wider. "I see how it is—letting the anticipation build up. You tease."

"That's right." Actually, it's because I suddenly forgot everything I have planned. I change the subject in an attempt to recover from my fumble. "So, how was your day?" I ask, leaning toward her and resting my chin on my hand, the picture of attentiveness.

We chat about work for a while. Or mostly, she chats about work, and I listen while trying to figure out how I lost my flow.

Why am I so nervous? Tonight will be exactly like all the other times we've fooled around. We're just having some harmless adult fun—and when we're done, our friendship will be there waiting for us on the other side, exactly how we left it.

But I can't silence the tiny part of me that knows otherwise.

Sex changes relationships. No matter what I keep telling myself, what we keep telling each other, that's how it works 99 percent of the time. It's not impossible that we'll come out of this fling exactly the same way we went in, but it's sure as hell unlikely. And I don't know how to feel about that.

The one thing I do know is I couldn't live with myself if I ever hurt her. Taking care of her heart is the absolute most important thing. So, maybe that's all I really need to focus on? But that's easy, right, not being a prick? I can do that.

Our food arrives, and I realize that Keaton has gone quiet. Shit, I've been lost in thought and ignored her too long. Bad date etiquette . . . no, this isn't a date. Whatever. Bad hangout etiquette, no matter who's involved.

"Hey," I say quietly.

She looks up from grinding pepper onto her food. "Hmm?"

"Are you sure you want to do this with me?" I hold her gaze steadily, wishing I could read her mind to see if she shares my uneasy thoughts.

"Of course." She sounds slightly confused. "You're the best person for the job. You've got experience, you know what you're doing, and I trust you to be honest and tell me if I suck." She snorts at her own unintentional joke. "I mean, the metaphorical, bad kind of sucking."

That isn't what I've been brooding over. But all I can do is let the point go.

"I'm glad to hear that," I say, and I genuinely am. At least it means I'm not fucking anything up . . . yet.

We eat for a few minutes in much more comfortable silence. Then I say, "For the record, you don't suck. Not even a little bit. You're amazing."

Her brilliant, slightly shy smile makes me think maybe everything will work out fine in the end, and I was worrying for nothing.

Then Keaton makes a low moaning sound as she tries her first bite of lobster macaroni and cheese, and all those X-rated thoughts come galloping back full force.

By the time we finish our meal, my cock has overtaken my brain, driving out all my worries and jitters. Now I'm just excited as hell to get us back to my bed.

I pay the bill, leaving a generous tip, then stand up to help Keaton from her seat. Her cheeks are slightly pink, and I can tell her mind is already on what will happen later too.

Outside the restaurant, I offer Keaton my arm. "Shall we?"

She giggles and grips my forearm, and I don't think I'm imagining that she feels just as revved up as I do.

The sun has set; the streetlights ignite one by one as we drive back to my apartment. When I let us inside, Keaton looks around with such interest that I have to ask, "What?"

She pauses, as if trying to figure out the right way to answer. "It's just, well, I've never seen your place so clean before."

I shrug, trying to downplay it. "Hey, now." But she's right—my normal housekeeping isn't nearly so impeccable. I spent hours yesterday cleaning up for her visit, and I'm glad she's impressed.

She stifles a chuckle. "Sorry. You asked."

I pull her close, murmuring into her ear, "You're going to pay for that comment."

"Promise?" Her voice is already husky.

I kiss her and she responds eagerly, her arms winding around my neck to pull me closer, to make me give her more . . . harder . . . hotter. Our tongues tangle in a fiery dance as we share quiet moans of pleasure and anticipation.

We can barely stand to break contact long enough to get into the bedroom.

CHAPTER
Eleven

Keaton

"**D**O YOU WANT ME TO TAKE OFF MY glasses?" We're sprawled across his bed already when the question slips out of me.

Slate doesn't stop kissing my neck, his lips still brushing the sensitive skin along my jaw as he murmurs, "Why would that matter?"

"I don't know." I laugh. "Just wondering what your preference is."

I remember the college boys who were always preoccupied with whether I wore them during sex or not. "Don't they get in the way?" they would ask, as if they were actually concerned with my personal comfort. Or then there were the enthusiasts, adamant that I keep them on the whole time. "You look like a sexy librarian," they would say, their eyes glazed over in whatever strange fantasy they were enjoying by themselves. Or worse, my ex-boyfriend who thought removing *his* glasses was the only foreplay needed.

My silly running thoughts fumble to a halt when Slate takes my face between his large, masculine hands. Between featherlight kisses on my cheekbones, hairline, and lips, he whispers, "Glasses or no glasses. Doesn't matter to me. I want you right now."

The certainty in his voice sends shivers of pleasure down my spine. This is a side of Slate I haven't seen yet. There are so many sides of him I'm seeing for the first time, like that rare moment of seriousness during dinner. I could sense that something was on his mind. I hope I calmed the brewing storm behind that furrowed brow. I thought I knew all of his sides before, but the more time I spend with him, the more of a mystery he becomes to me.

Fortunately, there isn't anything mysterious about the sensation of the tip of his tongue drawing soft lines along the top of my breasts. He's unbuttoned my blouse, revealing just enough cleavage for him to enjoy. My chest rises and falls with each labored breath; I can't help but get worked up over the feel of his affectionate touches. I've always had a very sensitive chest, so each breath and gentle press of his lips has my head spinning. I lift my hips involuntarily, my body naturally seeking his in a desire for more friction.

He's positioned on top of me, and I can feel his erection pressed against my hip, but just like the first time we made out on my bed, he's getting an A-plus in foreplay. Basically, he's driving me insane with desire, and I'm not even sure he knows it.

When I let out a soft, need-filled sound, something inside Slate's perfect self-control seems to snap.

Everything turns hotter, faster. Our fingers work at each other's buttons, and our own, to reveal more skin to drag teeth and lips across in a tantalizing search for our most sensitive spots.

He finds mine with little trouble, rubbing the tip of his nose over the satin of my bra. My nipple is fully erect beneath the fabric, waiting in anticipation for his touch. I arch my back and he takes the cue to unfasten my bra with one hand, while cupping one of my breasts with a firm squeeze in the other. His hands feel so good, so right. I can't help but anticipate how the rest of him will feel. My heart is pounding with excitement. I wonder if he can feel it under his fingertips.

The straps of my bra slide easily off my shoulders, and together we toss the garment aside. I pull at his shirt until we're both naked from the waist up, taking in the sight of each other's bare torsos. Slate is ripped, to say the least. His lean frame is accented by the unmistakable presence of muscle, a surprise to me as his number-one, brunch-binge buddy.

I run my fingers across the broad expanse of his shoulders, down his pecs and over his abs, loving all the firm muscles I find there. I've never done this before, never lingered with his body, and I'm enjoying it more than I ever thought possible.

Meanwhile, Slate feasts on the sight of my breasts. They're full and heavy, each topped with a rosy nipple—that are currently waiting to be touched by someone as skilled as Slate. He leans down, brushing his lips ever so gently across the tip of my right breast.

"Please, Slate." I moan, barely recognizing my own voice in its desperation.

"Yes, baby." His lips close over my breast in response, drawing my nipple into his mouth with a gentle suck.

I could scream aloud in sheer pleasure as his tongue draws languid circles around it. Slate moans in response to my enthusiasm, wrapping his arms tightly around me. He kisses across my breast bone to give my other nipple the attention it deserves.

I'm not concerned with fairness as much as I am with getting his pants off and squeezing that perfect ass between my naked thighs. I push him up, and it seems we're on the same wavelength, because we both begin pulling at the rest of each other's clothes, desperate to be bare, skin on skin.

His cock is just as I remember it, gorgeous and thick, with a vein on the underside begging to be licked. Before I can wrap my lips around its head to give it the good, hard suck it deserves for simply existing, he pushes me back onto the sheets. I land with a soft gasp, aroused by his change in demeanor.

Wild-eyed and with tousled hair, Slate really does look like some sort of god of desire. His cock presses gently against the soft, wet petals of my sex. What is he waiting for?

I look into his eyes, and the question is there. *Are you sure?*

I draw his lips down to mine in a long kiss so he can taste the answer on my tongue.

"Keat . . ." He breathes out my name as his firm cock kisses my damp center again. "Fuck. You feel so fucking good."

I wiggle beneath him, sliding my wetness along his shaft. I swear my brain short-circuits at how good that feels.

A sexy grunt tumbles from his lips and his eyes latch onto mine.

"Yes." I moan again, my hips still moving.

"You sure?" he asks, his eyes locked on mine.

"Very."

"Stay still for me."

I do as he says and watch as he quickly rolls on a condom. Then he clutches my hip in one hand as his other hand clutches the sheets by my head.

"If you don't like anything I do, if you want to stop—" He's cut off by my lips pressing to his in a firm kiss.

"Want you," I gasp, working my hips against him.

"Keaton," he growls.

Then inch by slow inch, he begins to fill me. I can barely breathe, thrown by how perfectly we fit; his girth sliding exquisitely against my tight walls.

"Fuck," he bites out once he's buried inside me.

He's right. It's completely overwhelming, yet so right at the same time. How is that possible?

My body grips his perfectly, and I press my mouth to his neck.

Slate draws back slowly, pushing in again, and the lowest, sexiest growl tumbles from his parted lips as I squeeze around him.

"You feel so good," he says with a groan.

We're both panting, our mouths open, gazes fixed on each other. His eyes spark in that way that they do when we've just exchanged an inside joke.

I don't think we could get any more inside than this, I think, a small smile tickling my lips. His own lips curl upward, and now we're laughing breathlessly at the perfection of our melded bodies. He drops down and gives me a soft kiss on my smiling lips. With a gentle nudge from my hips, he begins to move within me, faster now.

And my smile falls away.

The very air in the room shifts. I'm being tossed by warm waves of ecstasy, my wet sex pushing and pulling against his hard, confident length. I wrap my naked thighs around him, enveloping the pulsing muscles of his legs and ass.

"Tell me it's good for you."

My gaze meets his. "It's perfect."

His mouth is at my neck, kissing and nipping, and his breaths come in harsh pants. "You feel so tight. So damn good."

His words fill me with a sense of bliss, and everything he's doing feels amazing.

Being with Slate like this—it's better than I could have ever imagined. With every thrust, I'm threatening to come apart. His hot breath against my neck and his throaty murmurs are driving me wild. I imagined him being quiet during sex, but I like that I can hear every breath, that I'm the one making him groan out soft, need-filled sounds.

I meet him thrust for thrust, one of my hands combing wildly through his soft hair. My other hand is trapped beneath his, our fingers locked in a tight embrace above my head on the sheets. It's coming; we can both feel it. Slate's cock pumps harder inside me until the only thing that exists is him.

"Fuck, Keaton."

He moans against my ear and I'm lost, hurtling into an abyss of my own making. I shake with each gust of my orgasm, rocking against him so violently that he comes a second later. He pushes through the quakes, his cock still thrusting against my quivering walls.

I never want this feeling to stop. From the way he's repeating my name like a prayer, I don't think he does either.

Our orgasms finally fade, and I take a deep breath. The bed shifts as the sex god collapses next to me, our legs still entwined.

I open my eyes. I'm not sure when I let them shutter closed. Or when my glasses came off.

"Wow," I gasp. Between shaking breaths, I try to decide whether to just let myself melt into his sheets forever or attempt to be a functioning human again.

"Yeah," he murmurs back, half his face buried in

the softness of his bed as he lies, sated, on his belly.

I gaze at the way the sweat glistens on his back with every rise and fall of his breaths. Who knew this man was so damn beautiful beneath the sarcasm and jokes?

"I do feel like something was missing, though," he says out of the blue, propping his head up on one bent arm to meet my gaze.

My throbbing heart drops like a rock.

"What? Was it boring?" I ask, biting back any obvious signs of hurt in my voice. If he has comments on my sexual performance, I damn well want to hear them.

"Not at all." He smiles. "You are superb."

His hand cups my cheek in a surprisingly intimate gesture. I wonder briefly how our regular gestures and platonic nonverbals will change now that he has literally been inside me. Or rather, fucked my brains out.

"Then what was missing?" My eyes narrow, but my smile remains from the compliment. I can't help but glow a little. I don't think anyone has ever used the word "superb" to describe even my most impressive work on the job, let alone in bed.

"I guess I imagined our first time involving a lot more . . ." He trails off, as if struggling to find the proper word.

"Spit it out!" I smack his ass lightly.

"Cat hair." His expression remains thoughtful and distant, although his eyes sparkle with mischief. My heart leaps back into action, resuscitated by the normalcy of our usual banter.

"You are such an ass." I poke him on that very target for emphasis.

"You like it," he says with a grin.

I squeeze that supple muscle in response, not saying yes, but definitely not saying no.

"What time is it?" He flips over and stretches, not unlike how Penny does in the morning after a long night curled up on the duvet.

A few moments later, I'm back on my feet, fishing around for my cell phone in our pile of discarded clothes. I'm surprised I can still stand, to be honest. How amazing is it that I have such a great friend who happens to be amazing in the sack?

"It's almost eleven," I say with wide eyes. "I should go. Getting up for work tomorrow is going to be a bitch."

While I pull my shirt back on over my head, I hear Slate intake a breath, as if to say something. But he says nothing.

Working on my buttons, I ask, "What?"

"Nothing." He smiles, but I can tell it isn't nothing. What was he going to say? "I'll order you an Uber."

He launches off his bed, grabs his cell phone off the floor, and walks toward the kitchen, gloriously nude. Jesus, it's not fair how attractive he is.

He must feel me ogling the delicious curve of his backside because he asks, "Do you need some water to rehydrate from all that drooling?"

"I could use some rehydration, yes," I admit with a chuckle. *Busted.*

Why be embarrassed for getting caught staring at my best friend's ass? We just had explosive, life-changing sex, and I'm definitely not embarrassed about that. I feel incredible, still riding the high of the happy post-orgasm chemicals dancing across my brain.

And he's not acting weird, so why should I? *Don't overthink it, Keat.*

I take in the sight of Slate's bed, now thoroughly mussed from our romping. His room, like the rest of his apartment, is neater than I've ever seen it, except on holidays. I can't help but wonder what the occasion is.

Am I the occasion? That thought makes my belly flip.

"Uber will be here in two," he says, returning with two glasses of water.

He hands me one and sits on the edge of the bed beside me. We clink our glasses in familiar camaraderie and drink. I let my thoughts slide to the back of my mind with each refreshing gulp of water.

"I'll walk you out," he says, setting his glass aside.

"Like that?"

He looks down at his still flushed naked body. "I guess I should spare Maggie the Uber driver, shouldn't I?"

"Hmm." I flick water at his bare chest, enjoying how he jumps back with a little hiss. *Just like a cat,* I think with a smile. "Perhaps."

"You brat," he mutters, pulling his pants on. He reaches around me to grab his shirt off the floor, planting a quick, firm kiss on my cheek before turning toward the front hall. "All right, Little Miss Workaholic, let's get you home."

See? I tell myself. *Absolutely nothing has changed.* He's not acting weird, and neither should I.

I'm still smiling from our exchange when my car arrives. Slate helps me into the backseat. Time for good-byes. I'm expecting another high five or at least a fist bump.

I don't expect his hand to cup my cheek so gently

and his lips to press against mine in a soft, warm kiss. I don't expect to lean into that sensation, to draw his lips between mine in eager response. We linger like that . . . for just a moment longer than friends with benefits ought to.

When Maggie the Uber driver shifts in her seat and adjusts the radio, we get the hint and break apart. Slate's eyes have that giddy sparkle that completely gives away his happiness, and I wonder what my expression must look like to him.

The door closes, and Maggie and I are on our way down the road back to reality.

Okay, Keaton. Maybe something has changed.

CHAPTER Twelve

Slate

"HOLY CRAP, THIS PLACE IS PACKED," GABBY mutters as we walk into the bar.

She's not kidding—I can barely hear her over the chattering crowd, let alone the music, which is cranked to a twelve out of ten.

"Just another Saturday night downtown." I sigh in resignation. "At least there's still a few seats left at the bar. We won't have to split up."

Karina frowns. "No tables? *Ugh.* Those bar stools make my ass hurt. But I guess it's not the end of the world."

We wander toward the bar where I spot my friend Jack, who owns the place, and I give him a fist bump. "Hey, dude. Good to see you."

"You too," he calls out over the music.

The place is packed, and although he isn't usually working behind the bar, I guess I'm not all that surprised to see him here, helping pick up the slack.

"Business good?" I ask.

"Excellent." He nods. Then he gestures to the bartender beside him, getting her attention. "Get them anything they want tonight."

I shake my head, about to tell him that he doesn't have to do that.

"Hi, guys, sorry I'm late," Keaton calls out from behind us.

I turn. "You're not late. We just got h—" My mouth drops open.

Holy shit.

Keaton is wearing a wine-colored minidress that clings to her every curve. If I weren't so enamored with the way she looked in it, I'd want to throw a trench coat over the top of her just to keep anyone else from looking at her.

There are no sequins, or lace, or any other embellishments that most women prefer these days. But she doesn't need them. She's perfection. The plunging neckline shows off a dangerous amount of cleavage, and already I can feel my cock stirring.

Between the hem, which barely reaches halfway down her sleek thighs, and her black strappy heels, her legs look about ten miles long. *What the fuck?* When did Keaton's legs get so long? I'm about to ask her when I get ahold of myself.

Her long, dark hair is pulled back to show off her elegant neck and delicate collarbone before cascading down her back. Overall, her outfit is simple, but damn, is it ever effective—it lets her stunning body and face speak for themselves.

All I can say is, "Wow."

Gabby wolf-whistles loudly. "Ooh, look at you, girl! That dress should be illegal."

No kidding. I've seen Keaton all primped and polished before, and I certainly loved that dark pink number she wore on the first night we kissed, but this is on a whole other level of hotness. It doesn't help that I've already been distracted by her in new ways ever since we started hooking up.

I'll have to be careful not to let any boners make a surprise guest appearance tonight . . .

"I love it," Karina coos. "Is it new? Let me see the whole thing. Come on, do your little turn on the catwalk."

"Aw, thanks, you guys. I guess I just felt like sprucing up tonight." Grinning, Keaton twirls to show off, revealing how the dress bares her back all the way down to those twin dimples above her ass, and shows the perfect outline of her round backside.

Fuck.

My hands tighten into fists at my sides to keep from doing something stupid, like reaching out and touching her. I have to take a deep breath and convince myself not to drag her down the hall to Jack's office in the back and make her change.

"And no, it's not new. I bought it years ago and just never had the guts to wear it. I was so glad when it still fit." Then she gives me a small, sultry smile that only I can see, and a possessive heat stirs inside me.

I take a deep breath in an effort to calm myself. When we take our seats at the bar, I sit at the end of our little row, next to Keaton. I don't want any random douchebags creeping up next to her—with how incredible she looks, someone would definitely try it if I didn't play bodyguard. It's really just the gentlemanly thing to do.

The frenzied-looking bartender takes our drink orders and whips them out to us with impressive speed. Keaton's customary whiskey and Coke, followed by a tequila shot for Gabby, a vodka soda for me, and a mango mojito for Karina.

Normally, being out with the girls means I have built-in wing-women who other women seem to flock to—essentially making it easy for me to get laid. Tonight, though, that's the furthest thing from my mind.

Karina sips her drink with a loud sigh like she's just set down a hundred-pound weight. "Ah . . . it's so good to get out of the house and see you guys. I've been this close to losing my shit all week." She holds up her thumb and forefinger and pinches them together.

"What's Mateo doing now?" Keaton asks with an air of sympathetic weariness.

"Our wedding is practically tomorrow, so we should be done planning by now, right? But we're still arguing about the fucking guest list. I keep saying we don't have the money to invite his five billion cousins, not to mention the logistical nightmare."

Gabby squints in confusion. "Doesn't he hate most of his cousins? Why does he even want them there?"

"He does!" Karina groans. "The problem is, he's afraid his aunts will get their collective panties in a knot. And some bullshit about his inheritance. I think he should just let 'em whine. It's not like it's unfair if both of us invite only immediate family, but *no* . . ."

She continues venting, adding more swear words as she alternates between talking and drinking. But I don't hear the rest because Keaton has shifted to cross her legs, the hem of her dress riding up to expose a generous swath of upper thigh. The delicious glimpse draws my gaze like a magnet. I can't help myself, now that I know exactly how soft that creamy, secret skin feels, how surprisingly strong those legs are, wrapped around my back, pulling me deeper inside her . . .

Fuck.

"Hello? You there, Slate?" Karina says, prodding me.

I tear my gaze away. "Yeah," I say with a grunt.

She raises one eyebrow. "Really? Then what was I just saying?"

"Uh . . . your fiancé is trying to avoid family drama?"

Gabby giggles. "That's true, but we changed topics, like, five minutes ago."

Dammit. "Okay, you got me." I sigh. "Sorry. I was thinking about . . . this work problem." Hard work. Very hard. *Hard* being the operative word. I sneak another glance at Keaton's legs.

"You're really spaced out tonight." Gabby slurps her electric-blue cocktail. When did she even order that? I really haven't been paying attention.

"I'm just tired. It's been a long week." Especially because Keaton and I haven't had another chance to hook up since last weekend. So I'm horny on top of everything else.

I'm not ashamed to admit that I've grown accustomed to regular sex. Once or twice a week, I take a girl home from a bar to relieve the ache, but lately, that hasn't been the case. Because of Keaton. She's asked me to help her, and I'm committed to seeing it through. *And after last weekend* . . . I swallow.

Damn, that night was amazing. If I didn't know otherwise, I hardly would have believed it was our first time together. We were both so in tune with each other. I can't remember the last time I felt a connection like that. It was like we just knew—each other's bodies, how to move, anticipating what each other needed next.

And I was unimaginably turned on . . . my dick could have pounded nails.

Not only is Keaton gorgeous, but her responsiveness is such hot, wonderful fun. I could spend hours exploring her, learning what pleases her best, drawing out every possible erotic response. And watching her fumble with me, touching me in careful, measured strokes? The memory of it brings a smile to my lips even now.

I want to growl with impatient lust. A week is too fucking long to wait. I've spent every hour of every day itching to get reacquainted with her naked body. All I want to do is get Keaton alone again and make her squirm and scream and—

Gabby's voice interrupts my increasingly dirty reminiscing. "So tired you haven't noticed the hot blonde checking you out over there?"

"Huh?" I've barely heard what anyone has said, let alone spent any time trolling for tail. All I've done tonight is try not to get caught ogling Keaton.

Keaton points to the other end of the bar. "That one. She's been eyeing you up for, like, twenty minutes now." She cocks her head with a challenging smirk. "Go get her, Slate."

I shrug, not bothering to turn and see for myself. "Nah, I'm good."

Karina's eyes widen until they're comically large.

"Seriously, dude?" Gabby almost shouts. "There's a total babe staring a hole in your pants, and you're not even going to look at her? Or any of the other gazillion women here? Did aliens replace you with a robot clone?"

"Oh my God, you're right. He must be coming down with something." Karina reaches out to touch my forehead, and then my cheek. "Are you feeling okay?"

I bat her hand away. "Jesus, guys, I'm telling you I'm fine. Never better."

And it's true—there's been a spring in my step ever since Keaton and I added benefits to our friendship. But I can't say that. Keaton and I agreed to keep this private, just between us, and I'd never betray her confidence.

"Then why not walk on over there and work your magic?" Holding my gaze with hers, Keaton leans toward me, her elbows on the bar top. Her upper arms squeeze together slightly to deepen her cleavage.

Don't look at her tits, don't look, don't . . .

Fuck. I looked at her tits. And now all I can think about is that hot, whimpering sound she made when I sucked her nipples firmly into my mouth.

But I realize everyone is still staring at me, waiting for me to reply, and so I draw in a deep breath. "Because all I want to do tonight is chill with my friends."

Something touches my knee. Fingertips, circling.

Keaton? My eyes widen. *Wait, is she doing that on purpose?*

The touches continue, creeping up my thigh, making sure to brush the inside before withdrawing. Keaton winks at me.

I smirk to myself. Oh, it's on now . . . if she wants to play dirty, I'm down. When nobody else is looking,

I catch Keaton's eye and lick my lower lip, all slow and sensual, then bite it. Now she's the one who risks getting caught staring.

I keep my expression innocent, knowing my hand is hidden by the countertop as I reach toward Keaton and pinch one of the spots on her hip that I've learned is sensitive. She squeaks and jumps a little.

"Okay, what is *with* you two tonight?" Karina asks.

Oops. I guess our odd vibe is more obvious than I thought. Playing chicken is fine, but we can't totally give the game away.

"Nothing," we both blurt at the same time.

I cringe internally. *Smooth move . . .*

Karina shakes her head. "You're both drunk."

"Yes. Super drunk," Keaton says, nodding very seriously.

"Maybe you guys are, but I'm just getting started." Gabby stands up to catch the bartender's attention. "Next round's on me. Quick, what does everyone want?"

Keaton and I both say *thanks, but no thanks.* While Karina and Gabby are distracted with their drink orders, we flash each other a secret smile.

"Hey, when you're done with that, you wanna

dance?" Keaton nods toward my glass, which is mostly ice cubes at this point.

I take one last sip and stand up. "How about right now?"

"Perfect." With a heat in her blue eyes that I couldn't resist even if I wanted to, she takes my outstretched hand. She leans close to murmur in my ear, "And then what?"

Her husky tone sends wonderful shivers up my spine. "More dancing?" I play dumb, which makes her laugh and shake her head.

"After that . . . way after. My place or yours?" she asks.

My heart thumps harder, and chill bumps break out on the back of my neck.

Taking the risk of being spotted, I nip her exposed collarbone and relish her stifled moan. "Anywhere, any way you want, Keat. I can't wait to be inside you again."

Her cheeks flush and for a moment, I'm cursing myself, worried that I've gone too far, pushed her too fast.

But then I decide *fuck it, this is me.* This dirty side to me is one I've kept hidden from Keaton, but if she wants it—wants me—then this is part of the deal.

Keaton's lips part and her breathing quickens.

"You're trouble," she whispers.

I lead her out onto the dance floor. We grind and sway tightly together in a way I struggle to pass off as just two friends goofing around, until the music changes to a faster song and Gabby crashes into us, yelling, "Save some for me!"

I dance with Karina while the other two girls compete to crack each other up with silly moves . . . but my eyes are always, always on Keaton.

God, I can't wait until last call.

CHAPTER
Thirteen

Keaton

It's been two weeks since Slate and I began sleeping with each other, and it's been perfect, far more educational than I ever expected. But tonight he has something different planned for us, and I can hardly wait.

I check my phone for the time and smile. I'll be right on time. I tug at the hem of my cocktail dress, not enjoying the way my Uber driver's seats scratch and pinch my thighs. Maybe the tight, slinky dress with its open back and dipping neckline is a little excessive for tonight's events.

However, Slate insisted that I treat it like a "special goddamn occasion." Tonight is the night we explore the various sexual positions many women have already mastered: doggy, cowgirl, reverse cowgirl . . . the list goes on.

"And, of course, some classic sixty-nine to get

us warmed up," Slate said as I added item after item to my to-do list. I put three exclamation points next to this particular topic to remind myself to internet search the best tips of the oral trade.

There's plenty of fun to be had this evening. This, Slate has assured me. He's also insisted on paying for the entirety of the hotel room, calling it his "charitable donation" to my project. He wouldn't even let me dive into the Groupon wormhole as I normally would, had I been planning the evening.

Slate has come to call himself the benevolent Patron of the Sexual Arts. I would roll my eyes, but I'm too grateful to him for what he's helped me with so far. He really *is* my sexy patron saint. Not to mention it's a damn funny title.

Several hours of hygienic and aesthetic prep and here I am, on my way to some ritzy hotel suite I would have never booked for myself in all my years of planning business trips.

As we roll up to the building, I can't help but gape. *This hotel is way out of Slate's budget, isn't it?* I peer out the car window, taking in the ambient glow of the hotel lobby, the deep rose color of the interior design, the uniformed valet stationed regally at the entrance.

This is really, really nice, I think. *Too nice.* I

wonder if I can slip some money into Slate's wallet by the end of the night without offending him.

My phone rings. *Karina.*

"Hello?" I say, waving a polite good-bye to my Uber driver. The man gives me a once-over, blatantly passing judgment on me for what the obvious combination of my dress and destination means to him. S*ex.*

"Well, fuck you," I mutter as he speeds off. He's not wrong.

"Hi? What?" Karina responds, her voice surprised.

"Not you, the rude Uber driver. What's up?"

"I need someone to distract me from my own boredom. Mateo is out with his friends—honestly, thank God—and the only thing worth watching is reruns of *Ghost Hunt.* What are you doing tonight? Feel like a binge watch with me?"

Shit. "I'm, uh, busy this evening. I'm so sorry."

"Busy with who?" she asks. "Oh." Her mood suddenly shifts to something more playful. "Plans? Rhymes with . . . pecs?"

"Yes, yes, sex," I say, conceding. "And pecs, actually."

At the front desk, I press the phone to my chest so Karina can't hear when I quickly give the concierge

Slate's information. With a sweet smile, she offers me a key. The key card has a note tied to it with a ribbon.

What on earth? I open the small, folded paper.

Glad you could make it. See you soon, kitty.

The blush on my face is only deepened by the concierge's soft giggle. I'm going to beat him so badly for this.

Admittedly, I do appreciate the poorly drawn paw print in the corner of the paper. Slate is always equal parts sexy and humor. It occurs to me that that would be a great tagline for a dating-app profile. I'll have to suggest it to him later.

"Hello? Keaton! Sex with . . ."

"I'm hooking up with a coworker."

I don't know why I lie. Of all the people I should be able to tell about this, it's Karina, but for some reason I'd rather keep it to myself.

As the elevator doors close, I examine my make-up in the reflection of its metallic walls. No lashes out of place? Check. Lip liner? Still intact. *Good job, me.*

"Uh-huh," she says, unconvinced. "I won't ask any more questions. His place or yours?"

"That sounds a lot like a question. A hotel, actually. A really nice hotel." The door dings and I tiptoe out into the hallway, trying to get my bearings.

"A hotel? What the hell, Keaton, is he married or something?"

I nearly snort with laughter at the idea of Slate, our resident playboy, being married. Yeah, right. That will never happen.

"No, *God* no," I assure her. "It's all just for fun. We're changing it up."

I find the right door, insert the key card, and the lock flashes green. I have no idea what to expect on the other side. The door opens easily, and I hit the lights.

"Changing it up?" Karina gasps. "How long have you been seeing this guy?"

It takes me three full Mississippi seconds to readjust my jaw from its slackened gape.

"Not long enough for this."

The floor is covered in rose petals—absolutely *covered*. The smell is utterly intoxicating, and I inhale deeply. Slate has been sweet about my whole sexploration, but this is over the top. He's completely spoiling me.

I cover the microphone on my phone for a moment. "Slate?" I whisper down the short front hall into the room.

No response. He hasn't arrived yet.

I take a single step into the room, skewering a few petals with the heel of my shoe. Still reeling in utter amazement, I remove my shoes to avoid picking up any more petals. The flowers create a silken carpet beneath me. I can't help but shiver at the decadent way they feel under the soles of my bare feet.

"What's going on?" Karina asks, shamelessly begging for details.

She really is bored. I'll throw her a bone.

"I just walked in the room he booked for us. There are rose petals on every single surface."

"No way," she whispers, giddy with excitement. "That's so romantic!"

My pulse quickens as I find another note sitting on a nearby table, next to the crystal lamp. I almost rip the paper in my excitement to read it.

The hotel gave me two options for rose coverage: semi or full. Go big or go home.

The giggles hit me like an unexpected bear hug.

"What is that sound? Oh my God, Keaton, are you *giggling*?" Karina sounds concerned, which only makes me laugh harder.

"Yes. This is crazy!"

I can barely get the words out without the

unfamiliar sound bubbling out of me. It feels good to be this surprised. Who knew Slate had this in him? And, of course, he has to take it *way* over the top. I find myself loving this pleasant feeling inside me—this tantalizing taste of spontaneity paired with a deep fondness for Slate and all his lovable quirks.

Two emotions fill me in contrast—affection for my sweet friend who went to all this trouble, and the simmering heat of what tonight will hold. I release a breathy, little sigh.

Of course, *that* sound doesn't slide by Karina either.

"Who are you and what have you done with my surly mistress!" she cries over the line in mock distress.

"It's still me, don't worry." I pause. "Oh my God, this bed is massive! It's bigger than a king size. Is there a god size?"

The minifridge in the corner of the room catches my eye. I open it. Champagne, rosé, merlot . . .

"I don't think so. Who is this mystery man offering these romantic gestures?"

My breath catches. Are those chocolate-covered strawberries?

"A coworker, like I said." I can't help myself. I take a tiny bite of one strawberry, enjoying how the cool chocolate melts on my warm tongue.

"Right, right." She's not convinced, but she lets me get away with it for now. "Well, I'll let you go. Sounds like you've got a full night ahead of you, girlfriend."

I remember why she called in the first place.

"It's okay. I can talk for a minute. At least, until he gets here." I plant myself on the edge of the bed, sending more petals tumbling to the floor around my feet.

"No, it's fine. Enjoy your night. Besides, I don't think I've seen this episode of *Ghost Hunt*." I can hear her turning up the volume, the familiar intro music pulling me back to late nights drinking white wine out of coffee mugs in our little college apartment. "Have crazy sex, tell me all about it. I'll catch you up on the supernatural another time."

"I love you," I remind her. She knows, but it feels so nice to say.

"Love you too. Make sure you finish first!"

"Oh my God, 'bye." I laugh, and we hang up still giggling.

Maybe it's the lingering nostalgia of the *Ghost Hunt* theme song ringing in my ears, but I haven't felt this young in years. I throw myself back on the bed, enjoying how the flowers fly up around my body and float back on the duvet in a new pattern.

I turn my head to deeply inhale the scented bedding. My eyes flutter open, my smile growing as I spot a little black gift bag on the bedside table. I grab it and sit cross-legged on the bed as I reach inside.

There's a note in Slate's neat handwriting, but this one makes my skin break out in chill bumps.

Feel free to get warmed up. I can't wait to see what you've learned.

Inside the bag is a deep purple, subtly ribbed vibrator.

Whoa. That's . . . unexpected. But it could be fun too.

I peek at my phone. It's almost eight o'clock. Where is he? Maybe he's left another note.

I glance around the room and spot yet another piece of ribbon with a note attached, this time on the marble bathroom counter. I launch myself off the bed, excited to read what silliness he's left for me.

My blush creeps down to my chest, which only ever happens when I'm really excited. This creative side of Slate is fun in a new kind of way.

P.S. First, check out the tub. Jets!!

Two exclamation points? Adorable. It's so sweet how much thought he put into this.

The tub is expansive, easily taking up half of the bathroom. Bath salts, bath bombs, gels, and soaps galore line the edge of the tub. I don't really need a bath. I took a shower earlier, making sure all necessary surfaces were groomed to my liking. Taking a bath seems excessive . . .

But it *is* a *goddamn special occasion.*

In a matter of minutes, the tub is nearly full with a hot, steamy bubble bath. I've peeled off my slinky dress and piled my hair on my head in a somewhat graceless bun. Wineglass filled with bubbling champagne in one hand, I drag the fingertips of my other hand through the water to test the temperature. Perfect.

Sliding one foot and then the other into the tub is pure bliss. I lean back into the water, enjoying the way the heat steams up my glasses. Every work-related knot and ache unwinds in the almost-too-hot water, forcing the stress out of me.

I sigh as the nagging worry I had about the evening's expenses evaporate into the scented air. Slate was right. This is all worth it.

My fingers run slow, sensuous lines across my belly. I want to touch myself so badly. I think about

Slate's hands pressing against my hips, his lips dragging torturously across my breasts, his sparkling brown eyes flashing mischievously through thick lashes . . .

I reach for my phone and type a message.

```
Okay, you're right. The tub is great.
```

As I wait for Slate's response, another message occurs to me.

```
If you don't get here soon, I'll try
the jets without you.
```

Setting my phone aside, I feel my eyes getting heavy. If Slate doesn't get here soon, he's going to find my dead, waterlogged body. Cause of death? Too much relaxation.

I imagine him walking in, chuckling at the sight of my fogged-up glasses. He wouldn't hesitate at all to strip out of his clothes and join me. I wonder what he'll wear? Maybe a suit?

I try to remember a time when I saw Slate wearing anything other than business or brunch casual. I can picture how nice he'd look in a black suit jacket, emphasizing his broad shoulders. The sensuous embrace of his pants along the lines of his muscled thighs and calves. Would he wear a tie? I imagine reaching up a dripping hand to pull him toward the water, drawing his lips to mine . . .

I finish my glass of champagne, and then tiptoe naked and dripping across the room to refill it, hoping this isn't the moment he decides to arrive.

When I'm done with my second glass, I decide to get out of the tub. Wrapping myself in a fluffy robe, I grab my phone. It's almost nine!

I frown. Still no response from Slate. I dial his number. The phone rings six times before I hear Slate's voice.

"Hey, it's Slate. Leave a message if it's urgent. Otherwise, just text me like a regular person, you weirdo." *Beep.*

Well, buddy, you aren't answering your texts either. I hang up and begin to worry. What if something has happened? One more text. Surely, he'll respond.

`You can't spell Slate without`
`LATE, am I right?`

Three minutes tick by. Nothing.

I'm still damp, and now chilly, so I grab my

clothes, ditching the robe to stand before the mirror, naked. The girl staring back at me is wearing a sad expression. Hurt eyes gaze back from the mirror at the pathetic woman dripping on the tile.

Everything comes into focus at once. The reality of it strikes me like a cold, sobering slap.

I have feelings for Slate.

Otherwise, being ghosted wouldn't hurt this much.

"Fuck this," I say to no one. I can't let this happen.

Without even drying my skin off, I dress again in my costume. That's what it is, isn't it? Just a silken lie—alluring and fun, but not functional against the realities of life. I was pretending; *we* were pretending that this wouldn't happen to one of us.

I don't bother to empty the tub, just loop my strappy heels in my fingers on my way out the door. Catching feelings for a flaky playboy was the last thing I wanted on my to-do list, yet Slate managed to sneak his way into my heart.

With tears filling my eyes, I flee from the hotel room.

CHAPTER
Fourteen

Slate

THE SUITE IS DARK, QUIET, AND COLD WHEN I arrive around ten thirty.

I flip on the lights and call out. "Keaton?"

No answer. Hoping she just fell asleep, I walk through the suite to look for her. The bottle of champagne I had the bellhop leave on the table is half-empty. The perfume of bubble bath still hangs in the air.

She was here, all right . . . but not anymore.

My stomach sinks.

I check my phone and growl to myself at the multiple missed calls. It only gets worse when I read all her texts, which go from confused to clipped to seriously upset.

"Fuck," I mutter. She got sick of waiting for me and went home, and I really can't blame her. *She must think I'm a complete asshole.*

I have to call Keaton right now. I don't know what to say yet, but I have to apologize and try to make sure she knows I didn't just ditch her for no reason. Even if I can't get her to stop being mad at me, I don't want her to think I care so little about her.

Her phone rings and rings and rings. Pacing in tight circles, I pick up one of the many flowers scattered around the room, only to find that it's already started wilting.

Finally, my call goes to voice mail. Another bad sign . . . her phone is on, but she's not answering.

"Hey, Keaton, I'm so sorry, I didn't mean to stand you up," I rush to explain. "There was this huge clusterfuck at work. See, what happened was—" I cut myself off as I realize that if I were her, I wouldn't give a rat's ass about the details. "Never mind. It doesn't matter. What matters is, I know I should have called you sooner, but I just didn't get a chance. I'm so sorry—uh, I guess I already said that, but I really am, so . . ."

Shut the fuck up, Slate.

I tack on a hasty "please call me back" and hang up, wanting to punch the wall until something fractures.

I've ruined everything. I missed out on an amazing night with Keaton and broke her trust in the process. What the hell do I do now? Maybe if I text her, she'll see it? It probably won't help, but it's worth a shot.

I'm almost done typing a long apology when my phone rings and Keaton's name flashes on the screen. I almost drop it in my hurry to answer.

"Hello? Listen, I—"

"A work emergency?" Her tone is flat and icy. "And you couldn't have taken one single second to text me?"

My stomach flips, and not in a good way. It's amazing how much power her voice has come to wield over me in just a few short weeks. She can make my heart leap with her laugh, spark electricity to my groin with a husky murmur . . . or drip ice water down my spine with her displeasure.

"I know it sounds like a stupid excuse, but I'm not making it up." *Way to sound exactly like you're making it up, dipshit.* "I was fielding phone calls for three hours straight. I barely had a moment to breathe. The whole thing was a nightmare. Trust me, I would've much rather been here with you."

"Here? What . . ." She trails off as she figures it out. "You're at the hotel? Look, I'm not going to go back there now. It's already late, and I'm home in bed with Penny."

"I know," I say again, uselessly. "I'm sorry. I really feel awful for leaving you here alone without even telling you what was going on. Will you at least hear me out?"

Silence, followed by a sigh. "To be honest, I don't really want to talk to you right now."

Even though I saw that coming, it still feels like a kick to the nuts. "You don't have to. Can we meet up tomorrow?" Wait, no, that sounds like I'm asking for another bedroom rendezvous. I hasten to add, "I mean, for afternoon coffee or something." Totally not sexy, not a date, not anything approaching intimate. The words coming out of my mouth are at odds with the purple vibrator in my hands.

A very long pause. "I'm working late. I'll be busy until after six thirty."

"That's fine."

I'd meet her at three in the goddamn morning if it meant I had a snowball's chance in hell of salvaging this situation.

♡

When I arrive at the café we agreed upon, Keaton is already there, sitting at a small table in the corner.

Things already don't look promising. Hands in her lap, one leg crossed over the other so she's slightly turned to the side, and an untouched mug of tea sits in front of her. *Jeez, it's like I'm being interviewed.* It doesn't help that she's still in her stern business clothes.

She waits for me to sit down before she asks, without making eye contact, "So, just what was this work emergency?"

This is your one chance. Don't blow it. "One of my pro league players had a meltdown so bad, his coach checked him into rehab. I had to do damage control ASAP before the morning news cycle could get ahold of something they shouldn't."

Her eyes widen. "Oh my God. Is the guy okay?"

"Yeah, he's fine now. We'll have to see if the same is true for his public image. Even with all the work I did, I probably just made the impending media shitstorm a little smaller." I try again to look her in the eye and am relieved when she doesn't turn away. "Still, I could have—should have told everyone to fuck off for a second so I could text you. I feel like shit when I think about you waiting in that hotel. I'm sorry."

"Thank you." She gives me a small smile and even scoots a little to face me directly. But the atmosphere still feels weird. Withdrawn. Like we're sitting on opposite sides of the café instead of one little table.

I lean toward her, hoping she can tell I'm trying in earnest to fix everything, to put it all back the way we used to be. "What can I do to make this up to you? I could start by buying you another cup of tea."

She shakes her head. "That's sweet, but don't worry about it."

I blink. "Really? You sounded, uh . . ." *Homicidal.* "Pretty mad on the phone last night."

"Yeah, not gonna lie, I was super pissed. But I'm over it now." She shrugs. "I guess I just needed a little time to chill out."

"Are you sure?" I ask. "I mean, I'd totally understand if you—"

"Seriously, everything's fine. We're cool." With a note of finality, Keaton takes a long drink from her mug, her eyes downcast.

It doesn't feel fine or cool. I frown, studying her. I should be happy that she agreed to meet me at all, let alone forgive me . . . but something still feels off. Something has shifted between us. And I don't know what it is or what to do about it, so all I can say is, "Okay. Glad to hear it."

She nods with a pinched smile. For a few minutes, we just sit in awkward silence with nothing but the occasional quiet slurp to fill the cavernous space between us.

God, this is excruciating.

Needing someone to say something, anything, I try to joke, "I was afraid I'd totally fucked things up between us. Good to know it was only partially."

Her pained expression makes me instantly regret my half-assed attempt at humor. "Nothing is . . . you're not . . ." Keaton trails off.

Then why does it feel like I am?

She starts to reach across the table, hesitates, then rests her hand near mine, our fingertips barely touching. "Don't worry about it."

I try not to. It almost works.

CHAPTER
Fifteen

Keaton

"**G**ROSS INCOME IS THE TOTAL INCOME YOU make from work, without the taxes figured into—"

"I know what gross income means, young lady." Meera scolds me, swatting the air between us with an aged hand.

I'm helping my sweet-but-fiery little neighbor file her taxes again. This was a tradition I had accidentally initiated three years ago when I first moved into our apartment building. In a casual elevator conversation, she asked me about my evening plans. At the time, she naively assumed that I was as socially (and sexually) active as the women on her favorite sitcoms.

Reluctant to disappoint her but not brave enough to lie, I responded that I had an exciting date with my tax forms that evening. But taxes don't really bother me. In fact, I'm kind of a numbers person. Numbers make sense. They're neat and orderly, and behave like I expect them to. But ever since, Meera has coerced me into walking her through the process of filing taxes.

"Gross is just a silly word for it," Meera says. The wrinkles of her brow deepen in her frustration as I organize the paperwork neatly in front of us.

"You're right," I say with a smile. "The English language is strange like that."

I take another bite of coconut cake, enjoying the sweet and spicy flavors. This is our exchange. I help her with calculating figures, and she feeds me homemade Indian cuisine. It's the perfect transaction, really. I'm great with numbers and hate to cook for myself. She's terrible with numbers and is always seeking someone to fatten up. Win-win.

In truth, however, I don't mind doing Meera's taxes with her. This white-haired wonder has an entire lifetime's worth of wisdom. Sometimes her unsolicited advice regarding my personal life can be tiresome, like the time she gave me a shawl to cover my bare shoulders one summer morning she caught me before a jog. But she means well. With her children both living out of state and her husband gone, it's the very least I can do to drop by.

"Now, Meera, since it's been three years since your husband passed," I say carefully, "you can no longer file as a qualified widow. You'll have to file as 'single.' There will be less deductions, but I'll make sure—"

"Single!" Meera gasps. "He may be dead, but I am still married to my husband. That is ridiculous."

"I completely agree, but sadly, that's how the IRS wants you to file."

"Hmph!"

Her pout is absolutely adorable, as is her devotion to her late husband. It's sweet. But her next matter-of-fact comment stops me short.

"You should marry that man."

I sputter. "What man?"

"The nice breakfast man. He seems fond of you," she says, on a roll now. "And he'd be a good match. For tax purposes." With one finger, she pokes at the papers before us, smiling cheekily.

"I'll consider it."

I let Meera have her moment without a fight. It doesn't hurt anyone. The tingle in my chest certainly isn't uncomfortable, but I do my best to ignore it. I must be frowning because Meera's gentle hand finds my cheek.

"Why are you sad? Is he not a nice man?" The

concern in her dark, kind eyes is heart-wrenching.

"No, no. He's a nice man. He's just not, well . . ." I pause, considering how to explain the concept of a fuckboy to an eighty-year-old woman. I bet Gabby would know what to say. Only I haven't told anyone about Slate and me, which makes this all ten times more isolating. "He's not *reliable*."

"So he made a mistake and hurt you." She nods, understanding in some impossible way.

"I guess so." I shrug. I don't really want to get into the specifics. Her husband is gone and her children are neglectful. No way do my problems measure up in the slightest.

"Is this the first time he has made this mistake?" she asks.

I furrow my brow, trying to remember through our years of friendship if Slate has ever truly let me down before.

"I guess it's a first," I find myself saying. "I don't think he's ever done this before."

"Then you must forgive him," she says, patting my hand lightly. "Forgive him and let him become a better person. Or you will never grow, separately or together."

Meera's words follow me out of her apartment and into the hall after her taxes are complete. Maybe she has no patience for finding the best deductions, but she has the patience to listen and dole out advice. She's a perceptive old woman, that's for certain.

Slate messed up once and I let myself take it personally. Losing him as a friend would be a mistake, even if that means ignoring my feelings. It isn't like he forced me to have these feelings. I acquired them, and I can just as easily get rid of them. Then we can go back to how it should be—Slate and Keaton, best friends. *Just* friends.

I open the door, anticipating the meowing of my irritable roommate, demanding to be fed. Strangely, she doesn't come pitter-pattering down the hall in her usual rush to greet me, Bringer of the Food. She must be fast asleep, most likely on my pillow or in my underwear drawer. That little lady has no respect for boundaries, I swear.

Into the kitchen I go, now on complete autopilot. I scoop up Penny's food and dump it in her dish, followed by a fresh bowl of water. My mind wanders back to Slate.

The way he always made me feel so comfortable, even when we were exploring uncharted territory together. The way his mouth would quirk up in a playful smile when I said something that amused him. It's crazy the things you can miss about a person.

I realize I've been squatting on the floor over Penny's food dishes, lost in thought. Where the hell is that cat?

"Penny! Food!" I call.

It's a bizarre thing to say, since I've never had to remind her about her favorite part of the day. Slate mentioned the same had happened to him when he was on Penny Patrol. He'd found her in my room, so that's where I go.

My room is dark and depressing. I yank the curtains open and the sunlight streams in, warming my skin. My foot lands on something soft.

"Oh my God, Penny! Sorry!"

I've stepped on her tail. She's sprawled out on the floor, half beneath the edge of the curtain, half illuminated by sunlight. She must have fallen asleep here, craving the rays after being confined in this dark room. I instantly feel terrible. Just because I didn't want to see the sunlight doesn't mean she should have missed out.

"Don't be mad," I croon, reaching down to scratch her butt. The little monster loves her butt scratches, and that's usually enough to win her back after an accidental tail-stepping.

She doesn't move.

My heart thumps with panic.

"Penny?"

♡

The doorbell rings. My eyes, red and teary, crack open.

I'm curled up on the floor in my room, next to Penny. The small patch of sunlight is gone, and the carpet feels cold against my skin. I must have dozed off, my cell phone resting limply in my hand. It's been about forty minutes since I called Slate, barely coherent through the sobs. I hear the door open.

"Keaton?" His voice travels down the hall.

"We're in the bedroom," I croak.

I'm glad I thought to leave the door unlocked. The last thing I want to do is leave Penny. I run a finger along the soft padding of her paw. She would never let me touch her perfect little paws before . . . It feels intrusive, like I'm taking advantage of her. I curl my hand up in a fist, punishing myself with the sharp dig of my nails into my palm.

The door creaks open. Slate takes a sharp breath at the sight of me curled up on the floor next to my dead cat. He holds his breath before releasing it in a deep sigh.

"Hey, Keat," he says, his voice like a soft blanket.

I want him to cover me with his softness.

My eyes fill with tears. I don't look at him. "Hi." My voice sounds unfamiliar to my own ears, distant and broken.

He enters my line of sight, kneeling beside me. His eyes are full of emotion as he stares at Penny's lifeless body. He reaches out a tentative hand to brush the hair off my tearstained face, then he helps me up into a seated position. Without asking, I lean my head against his collarbone, needing something firm to keep me grounded here in the moment.

"Do you know what happened?" he asks.

"No." I sniffle. "I just found her like this. I left the curtains closed. I never do that because I know how much she likes the sun."

"Keaton, this isn't your fault," he says softly, tucking my hair behind my ear. "She was old, and she lived a good life."

"I know." I sigh. "But it still feels terrible."

Slate kisses me softly on the crown of my head. I soak in the compassion of the gesture through my whole body.

"I'm going to take care of her, okay?"

"Okay."

♡

About an hour later, I'm still on the floor. Only now I'm in the kitchen, sitting cross-legged on the tile. Before me waits Penny's dinner, untouched.

The tears simply won't stop. I didn't know I had this much water in me. After Slate left to take sweet Penny to be cremated, I pulled myself up off the floor and came in here to make some tea. Now the tea is cold, over-steeping in a mug on the kitchen counter.

I remember how gently he lifted Penny off the carpet, how carefully he wrapped her in a soft sheet, and how softly he placed her body into the box. It was a shoe box for a pair of boots I impulse-bought online. I could have spent that extra money on healthier food for Penny, or maybe taken her in for a checkup. I hadn't taken her to the vet in a while. Why hadn't—

The front door creaks open. He's back.

"Keaton? Where are you? Oh, hey." He spots me on the tile. The box is gone. "You're on the floor again."

"Yeah." I sniff, wiping the residual snot from my sore nose.

Slate pulls some napkins off the table and offers them to me. When I don't take them, he carefully wipes my nose with the softest corner he can find.

"There."

"Thank you." I sigh. I'm a mess. I can't even look him in the eye, so I just place a hand on his closest knee.

"Hey, just a little snot. No biggie."

I can hear his smile. I would smack his arm if I had the energy.

"No, I mean, for taking her—"

"I know, Keaton." He places a soft, tender kiss on my forehead.

A strangled sob escapes my throat, shaking my whole body. He wraps his arms firmly around me, holding me upright as if I'll turn to dust if I let myself collapse to the floor. I fall deeply into the embrace, leaning my entire body weight on him. Both our bodies shudder with the quaking of my grief.

"I came in here—to—make tea." I try to speak through the gasps. "But then—her food—she didn't—"

"Just breathe," he reminds me when the hiccups begin to choke me.

Like a good coach, he takes me through the motions. His broad chest expands with a breath, and I follow his lead. Together, we exhale. Over and over, I breathe in through my nose and out through my mouth, doing my best to steady myself against the storm twisting my insides into knots.

"That's right. You're doing great."

Just as it feels like I'll never steady again, the sobs subside. Slate rubs deep circles on my back, grounding me more in the here and now. I may not be able to show it, but I'm so glad he's here. Even his familiar scent is comforting.

He must be trying to distract me because he casually says, "Looks like you made yourself some tea?"

"It's cold now."

"That's okay. Let's get you in bed. I'll bring you a fresh cup."

I look up at him through swollen eyes, amazed by how capable he is in my state of helplessness. I don't know how to handle myself like this. I'm always the calm-in-crisis friend. The rock. The anchor. Now I'm the one who needs someone to help me to my feet, walk me to my bed, tuck the covers underneath my chin, and bring me a cup of warm tea. Slate does exactly that, all with the gentleness of a true friend who doesn't ask anything in return.

"What are you thinking about?" He sits on the edge of the bed as I sip on the tea he's brought me. The familiar scent of lemon, chamomile, and ginger fills the room. *Tension Tamer.*

"This tea. It's my favorite." I smile at him, my expression quizzical. "How did you know?"

"The cover art on the box is a badass princess sitting on top of a dragon." He grins. "It was a pretty easy assumption to make."

I let out a snotty laugh, which is extraordinary given the circumstances. Then I take another swallow, deeper this time. The warmth of the tea whispers and caresses the knots of my gut into relaxation. My heart still sits heavy in my chest, but at least I can breathe again.

"Thank you for being here," I whisper. My gaze lingers on the spot on the floor where I found Penny, just over an hour ago. I can't decide whether the time lapse feels like years or seconds.

"There's no place else," he responds simply. His hand grazes mine, and I catch his fingers desperately in my own. We're the only two people in the world in this quiet moment.

"Do you want to take a bath? I can run one for you."

I shake my head. "Will you stay with me a little longer?"

"Of course."

Slate, my hero for the day, my savior, lies down beside me. He lets me pull his arm around my body, snuggling in close. There are no questions asked, just his firm body pressed protectively against mine.

As my tired, heavy eyelids droop from the weight of the day, one uncensored thought slips out in a soft whisper. "I'm so lucky."

Is it to myself? To him? To the world? I don't know, but with that sighed truth, I fall deeply, peacefully asleep.

CHAPTER
Sixteen

Slate

"ARE YOU FREE THIS SATURDAY AFTERNOON?" I ask Karina, holding my phone with one hand and typing on my laptop with the other. I've already sold my basketball tickets for Saturday's game to a Craigslist scalper to make this event happen and not be out any money. Now I'm searching for a good, decently priced florist. Figuring out refreshments will have to wait until I get a guest head count.

"Not really. Why, what's going on?"

Maybe I'm just stressed out, but Karina already sounds skeptical.

"Well, Penny died yesterday, so . . ."

"Oh no!" she says with genuine sympathy. "Keaton must be so upset."

"She really is."

Remembering Keaton's tears makes my heart

188

clench tight. When she called yesterday, she sounded so broken. I didn't even wait for her to tell me what had happened; I just grabbed my keys and hauled ass to my car.

"So I'm organizing a memorial service. It'll be at Keaton's apartment, and I was thinking around three o'clock, but the time is flexible depending on when people are available."

A long pause. "Like a funeral? For a cat?"

"More like a wake, but whatever. Look, I know it sounds silly when I say it out loud, but Keaton is really broken up about this, and I wanted to do something to support her. I figured if we all got together to remember Penny, maybe that would help give her closure."

"Uh, hmm, I don't know, I have a ton of wedding stuff to do this weekend . . . and, well . . ." Karina's waffling fades away into uncomfortable silence.

"Well, what?" I say, trying not to snap.

"It's not like Penny even liked me anyway." Karina hesitates. "To be honest . . . not to disrespect the dead or anything, but did she even like Keaton? She always acted so mean."

"Oh, come on, she's just a cat. Was a cat. We can't—" I correct myself. "Actually, so what if she was a total asshole? Memorials are for the living. What matters here is showing *Keaton* we care about her feelings. And right now she needs her friends."

"Look, I'm really sorry to hear Penny died, and I'll call Keaton to send my regards as soon as I get off the phone with you. But I already said I'm going to be busy all weekend."

"I promise it won't take long. All you have to do is show up at her place and say something nice about Penny."

"And how the hell am I supposed to do that? The last time I saw Little Miss Demon, I almost never saw anything else ever again, and do you know why?"

"Karina, just—"

"Because she went straight for my eyes! So even if I had time, which I don't, what nice thing could I possibly say?"

"I don't know, it's supposed to be *your* memory of Penny. If you really can't think of a compliment, then I guess just say literally anything you remember about her that doesn't involve bodily harm." I rub my forehead, trying not to sound so frustrated, and drop my voice to a pleading tone. "Please, Karina? This would mean so much to Keaton. There'll be free food and drinks, and you can leave after five minutes if you want."

"That's great, but you're not listening to me. I

have to confirm times for all our vendors and drivers, review the RSVP list and finish assigning seats, get my hair cut and colored, send a billion payments. And I've been procrastinating on writing my vows, and—"

I didn't want to resort to a guilt trip, but Karina's forced me to bust out the big guns. "Remember your cousin's baby shower?"

Judging by her heavy sigh, she definitely does. "Slate . . ."

"When the caterer canceled, and Keaton stayed up all night baking four dozen cupcakes?" I press on, not giving Karina an opening to object again. "You owe her big-time. She's been an awesome friend to all of us for, what is it, ten friggin' years now?"

"All right, all right," she huffs. "I'll figure out how to move things around somehow. Christ on a cracker." Then her tone softens. "I hope this helps Keaton feel better. Even if I don't understand why, she really did love that cat."

"Thank you. I'm sure it will."

I hang up, realize I've been pacing, and sit back down at my desk. Only six more calls to go . . . and given the Late Great Penny's charming personality, I've got a feeling I'll have to work just as hard for every single RSVP.

But if organizing this thing can get Keaton to smile again, the hassle will all be worth it.

♡

I survey my work with satisfaction. Keaton's living room is all set up for the wake, and I handled every detail. Well, she insisted on helping me clean her apartment, but everything else was all me.

Near the front door, I've set up a long table offering a selection of drinks and finger foods. On the opposite wall stands a smaller table with the urn holding Penny's ashes, a framed photo of her, and a potted white orchid—the florist suggested something that Keaton could keep longer than a few days. I've also put folding chairs facing the couch in a semicircle.

Meera is the first to arrive, five minutes before three. She presses a wide bowl of syrupy, reddish-brown dough balls into Keaton's hands. "Hello, dear. I'm so sorry to hear about your loss. Have you been eating well? Take some of these."

"Oh, thank you. It looks delicious. Um . . ." Keaton looks around for a place to put it.

I shove aside dishes on the already crowded snack table to clear a spot. "Here."

Before I can help them set out Meera's food,

someone else knocks, and I have to go answer the door.

It's Gabby, with a gold-wrapped package tucked under her arm. "Hi, Slate," she says before calling to Keaton, "How you holding up, babe?"

Still at the refreshment table, Keaton says, "Neither of you had to bring anything, you know. I would've been happy just to see you."

Meera frowns. "Nonsense. I couldn't come empty-handed to say good-bye to Penny. And I know *gulab jamun* is your favorite."

"What she said," Gabby chimes in.

"All right, all right." Keaton shakes her head, but she's smiling.

Soon Karina arrives, also bearing a gift. More and more of our friends trickle in over the next half hour.

As the room gradually fills up, Meera looks out of place, a little old lady surrounded by people in their late twenties and early thirties. Once everybody has helped themselves to snacks and drinks and found a seat, Keaton and I take our places on the couch, and I clear my throat to get everyone's attention.

"Thanks for coming. We're gathered here in memory of Penny," I say, trying for a casual, yet heartfelt tone. "She lived a great life with her loving owner, and passed away peacefully in her sleep at the age of seventeen. She will be greatly missed. We'll all remember her beautiful orange coat and her . . ." *Lust for destruction.* "Proud, spunky spirit."

Hoping I'm not making this sound ridiculous, I sneak a glance at Keaton, only to find her eyes brimming. *Okay, she's into it, which is all that matters. Let's forge ahead.*

"Now, let's all go around and share a memory of Penny." I look at Karina, the next person in the circle.

Karina passes her gift to Keaton. "Go on, open it."

Keaton obeys, revealing a bottle of pink nail polish. She gives Karina a questioning look.

"The color is salmon," Karina says. "Because salmon was Penny's favorite food, and it reminded me of her."

"Oh, I get it." Keaton smiles at her. "Thank you. I'm amazed you even knew that."

Karina shrugs, grinning back. "You talked about her a lot."

"Me next!" Gabby hands over her gift. "I found a pair of fuzzy purple slippers like the ones Penny ate last year."

That actually manages to get a laugh out of Keaton.

We continue around the circle, each friend

sharing a cute anecdote and sometimes a small memento related to Penny.

Finally, we reach Meera. "I remember when you first came to live here," she says. "I could hear Penny the moment you stepped out of the elevator with her carrier. All the way down the hall to your door, yowling, growling, just so angry! So offended—*how dare you move me*, she said!"

Keaton lets out a waterlogged giggle, and Meera's smile deepens the crow's feet around her dark eyes.

"But as soon as you put the key in the lock, she stopped. Like she knew this was her new home. This was where she was supposed to be."

Keaton gives a loud, wet sniff. "Aw, Meera . . ." She blows her nose and takes off her glasses to wipe her eyes.

"That's a really sweet story," I say truthfully.

I didn't expect to actually feel moved today—I thought our little get-together would be all about Keaton—but even the people who hated Penny are smiling despite themselves.

♡

Our guests linger for another hour or so, finishing their snacks, talking with Keaton, drifting away one by one until the apartment is empty. I start cleaning up the refreshment table, packing leftovers and wiping up spills and stray crumbs. Keaton joins me, so close our elbows brush as we work.

After a few minutes, I hear a quiet sniffle and look up at her. "You okay?"

"I don't know what to say, Slate. I really needed this. I didn't even know how bad I needed it until you . . ." Her voice quavers and she looks away, blinking rapidly but smiling. "Thank you so much for organizing everything. You didn't have to."

I give her a quick squeeze. *You're welcome* doesn't seem adequate. "It's like Meera's story about Penny. I knew this was where I was supposed to be."

As soon as I say it, I realize it's true. And not only when Keaton is sad and needs comfort. In every mood, in every situation . . . I belong by her side. It's where I feel the most right.

Oh shit.

A knot forms in the pit of my stomach. It's in that instant I know.

I'm falling for her.

I turn back toward the table, trying to stay totally focused on cleaning. This was absolutely not in the plan. We were supposed to just be fooling around, giving Keaton a chance to practice and get more confident in bed. We assured each other over and over that sex wouldn't change our friendship.

Well, falling for someone is a pretty big damn change, isn't it? *You idiot. Now what the fuck do I do?*

If she doesn't feel the same way, telling her will make everything weird. Even if she does share my feelings—not that I can allow myself to consider the possibility—then what happens next? Could anything even work between us? She practically lives at the office.

As for me, settling down has never been on my horizon. Staying casual has worked out great for my whole adult life. Just enjoying life to its fullest, always open to whatever adventure comes along next. Can I really give that up? Would I even be a good boyfriend? Would I live up to Keaton's expectations?

Look what happened with Tanya. Hell, look what happened with Mom and Dad. Those are the only two outcomes I've ever seen—either a relationship makes you miserable, or it's amazing and then fate rips it away and you end up miserable anyway.

Still, I can't shove down these feelings and pretend they don't exist.

I keep my eyes downcast, afraid of what my face might reveal, even as I can't bear to step away from her.

"So, um . . . do you have plans tonight?" she asks. There's a hopeful look in her gaze, like she wants me to stick around.

And really? There's no place I'd rather be.

"Not really. If you feel up for going out later, we could go out to dinner," I say. While I wait for her to answer, I toss the rest of the trash into the can.

"Slate," she says quietly.

I turn to look at her and am struck by the look in her eyes—the naked vulnerability and gratitude that pins me to the floor. "Yeah?"

She leans ever so slightly closer. "Well, I . . . I have some ideas for how to thank you for today."

I almost tease her for forgetting that she already thanked me. Then I realize what she means, and my mind threatens to go blank. "Oh. Um. You don't have to do that." Sex is the last thing on my mind right now. I just want to be here for her, and help any way I can.

"But I want to." Her face is barely an inch away now. And then—

Keaton's kiss is gentle and soft, but so needy I find myself kissing her back, wrapping my arms around her, helpless to hold back all the tenderness I feel for her. I need to give her everything; I couldn't say no even if I wanted to. She lets out a happy sigh, as if she already knows that.

We part slowly. Smiling at me, she takes my hand and leads me into her bedroom.

My heart pumps out an uneven rhythm. If this is how she needs me—shit, I'm game.

CHAPTER
Seventeen

Slate

WE STRUGGLE TO UNDRESS EACH OTHER while locked in a deep kiss. But being with her like this feels so good, I don't want to stop. I lie back on the bed, letting my eyes rake over her bared body, and grin when I catch her ogling me in the same way.

"Get that gorgeous ass over here," I say. "Come ride my cock."

We didn't get to try out girl-on-top at the hotel, or any other new positions for that matter, and I want to make up for the chance we never should have missed.

She purrs with enthusiasm and climbs onto the bed to straddle my hips. My breath hitches as her already-wet pussy brushes the head of my straining cock. It's in that moment I remember I'm supposed to be teaching her, trying to impart some wisdom.

"Come here. Tease me a little first."

Keaton pauses, considering, then rolls her hips down, rubbing herself against my rigid shaft. She lets out a sigh of slight relief at the friction. She keeps grinding on me, stimulating herself while slicking up my cock with her own juices.

My breath hitches in my throat as I watch her move experimentally. Pushing up onto my elbows, I guide her mouth to mine, and we kiss deeply as Keaton continues her sweet torture.

Finally, when neither of us can stand the wait anymore, she sinks down onto me. We both groan as her wet heat slowly envelops me. It seems like an eternity before my cock bottoms out inside her and her pelvis rests completely on mine.

She lifts up, then slides back down, pulling a gasp from both of us. Then again, with more force, and again, soon finding her rhythm. I brace my hands on her hips to guide her body above mine.

She cries out when my fingers touch her clit. She rides me faster and faster, plunging herself up and down on me, moaning every time I strike that sweet spot inside. I rub her clit faster and buck up harder to meet her thrusts. I'm desperate to make her come; I need it more than my own release, my own breath. I'm drunk on the sight, the sound, the scent of her, how stunning she is in her passion. And when our eyes meet, a wave of tenderness and desire threatens to drown my heart.

She throws her head back. "Oh, Slate . . . oh, *oh*, I'm gonna—" Her words dissolve into a wordless moan.

Her inner walls clench around my cock, nearly pulling me over the edge with her. Through the blinding pleasure, I struggle to keep rubbing her clit, wringing every last drop of ecstasy out of her orgasm until she whimpers with overstimulation.

She stills above me, her eyes half-lidded and hazy on mine. "Did you finish?"

I shake my head. Honestly, my only goal was to make her feel good. After the couple of days she's had, it was the least I could do. "Do you want me to?"

"Of course I do." She lifts her hips again, this time with trembling thighs.

I toss her an amused smile and shake my head. "Let me drive."

I help Keaton from her spot, and she lies down next to me. Then I move between her legs and hitch one slim calf around my hip as my cock, still straining and rigid, finds her warm center. She's tighter after she comes, and when I work myself inside again, the exquisite feeling steals my breath.

"Fuuuck." I growl, pumping harder as Keaton moans softly. It's the look in her warm gaze as she watches me take my pleasure that finally undoes my self-control. Soon I'm pinning her hips to the bed with mine and filling a condom with hot semen that jets out of me almost violently.

For a moment we just lie there together, panting, the sweat of our exertions cooling us off, still riding the high of incredible sex.

When I disentangle and lie beside her, she rolls over bonelessly and pillows her head on my shoulder. "Mmm, you're warm," she mumbles into my chest.

I smirk at her, even though she can't see it from her angle. "You falling asleep on me?"

"Not yet." She cuddles closer, pressing her naked body flush against my side, and drapes her arm over my waist.

It's crazy how normal this feels. How right. How perfect.

I caress her shoulder, then down over her side and the curve of her hip. She gives a soft murmur of bliss, so I do it again, and again, and again.

Gradually, the post-orgasmic euphoria mellows into a happy peace. I could keep up this slow, steady petting for hours, just to hear those soft sounds of her contentment. I sigh deeply and catch the lavender scent of her hair. As I look down at her serene face, her long, sooty eyelashes resting on her cheeks, the corners of her mouth upturned ever so slightly, I can't help smiling.

Dammit. I really do have feelings for her, don't I?

My worries from earlier creep back to the front of my mind. I can't procrastinate on this decision forever. I can either tell her about my feelings . . . or quash them and hope they eventually go away on their own. The latter idea is unbearable, and the former drives me crazy imagining all the ways everything could go wrong.

Then again, I'm not an oracle. I can't actually predict for sure how anything will turn out. There's no point in trying to look into the future and plan every step I take, because we never know what tomorrow will bring. That's why my attitude has always been to just live in the moment.

Hell, if I look at this situation a different way, that philosophy is even more reason to be honest with Keaton. What if one of us got hit by a bus or something before I could fess up? The future isn't guaranteed—what happened to Dad taught me that.

So maybe I should try to chill out and approach

this one step at a time. Don't overthink it. Just lay it all out in the open, and whatever happens . . . will happen.

Even if my feelings turn out to be totally unrequited, romantic rejection isn't the end of the world. We're a couple of mature adults who can figure out how to get over this temporary awkwardness and stay friends. Besides, I've always known Keaton to be kind and sensitive; I trust her to let me down gently. She isn't like Tanya. She won't twist the knife.

Now I just have to muster up the balls to do it.

I take a deep breath. "Hey, Keaton?"

"Hey, Slate?" she echoes teasingly. Her tone is playful, sleepy, a little husky. A bedroom voice that brings back every moment of the incredible evening we just had. When I don't answer right away, she props herself up on her elbow to look at me. "Yeah?"

God, she's so beautiful. How do I do this? Why is talking about feelings so damn hard? Just get it over with. Open your stupid mouth. Come on, Slate, pull it together and *say it!*

"I know this isn't what we talked about—" The words spill out in a nervous rush. I clam up again, trying to slow my suddenly clumsy tongue, but my hammering heart makes that feat hopeless.

"Huh?" She looks like she can't decide whether

to laugh.

"Well, uh, I think I might be starting to . . ." *Stop waffling and spit it out.* "Fall for you."

Her gentle smile fades to a blank stare. "What?"

Holy shit, I didn't think this could get any more stressful. What does she mean, *what?* How else can I say it?

"I mean . . . I'm falling in love with you."

She blinks. Then silently, she sits up. My side feels cold where her body was pressed against it.

"Keaton?"

No answer. She just stares off into space, her brow creased in an expression I can't read. Upset? Scared? Angry?

"Say something," I say, trying not to sound like I'm panicking.

She turns her face away. "Oh, Slate . . ." Her voice quavers. "No, you aren't."

Now it's my turn to gape at her. "What?" I knew there was the possibility that she'd reject me, but what the fuck is this? She's telling me that what I'm feeling isn't what I'm feeling . . . who the fuck does that?

Her hand twists tight in the bedsheets. "You don't love me."

My mouth opens and closes a few times, speech-less. "I . . . you . . . h-how can you say that? How can you tell someone else how they feel?"

"Because I know you, Slate!" Her voice threatens to crack. "And love isn't you. It's not at all what you're about. Especially not loving me. We're friends. Friends who have had some great sex, but friends. That's it."

I grab her shoulder, trying to turn her, to see her face, to grasp at even the smallest hint of what's going on in her head, and I feel sick when she flinches. "What are you talking about? I'm me and you're you, and I just told you I love you. So—"

She shakes her head rapidly. "I mean you're not the kind of guy who settles down with a steady girlfriend. This is just the first time you've had sex with someone you actually care about. And that's great, I feel so much for you too, but let's not confuse this for something it's not."

My stomach tightens. "Something it's not? So, what *is* it, then? Because I know how friendship feels, and I can tell this is way more than that—and we both know it. You can't put me back in the friend zone when we've already blown way past those boundary lines, Keat."

There it is. All out in the open, just like I intended. But it doesn't feel like a weight off my shoulders. It feels like I've puked in front of her. Like an ugly mess I've thrown down between us, pushing us apart, when all along we promised that what we were doing wouldn't dim the brilliance of our friendship.

"Now who's telling whom what they feel?" She presses her lips together in a thin, tight line, frantically blinking back tears. "Dammit . . . I didn't want things to turn out this way."

"Well, neither did I," I can't help snapping.

"I never meant to lead you on, Slate. I didn't want sex to change us. I just . . . I want my friend back." She sounds just as small and miserable as I feel.

I can't take this awkward feeling between us anymore. I get up and start yanking my clothes back on. "I have to go."

Behind me, I hear a stifled sob.

"I'm sorry," she whispers.

"I can't. I just . . . I can't." I don't look back at her pleading eyes because I don't want to see what might be reflected in them.

As soon as I'm dressed, I'm out the door, feeling like absolute shit.

♥

I barely remember driving back home. Numb, I get myself ready for bed like I'm piloting an unwieldy robot.

I trusted Keaton. I thought I knew how she'd react. Her denial—not rejection, her denial that I even have real feelings for her at all—totally blindsided me.

How the hell did this happen? Have I been fooling myself all along? Was I just imagining the powerful connection I thought we had?

Keaton's words keep spiraling around my mind so fast I feel sick. *Not the kind of guy who settles down with a steady girlfriend.* I mean, it's true that I've only had one girlfriend, and she was over ten years ago. But just because I'm not very experienced in that department doesn't mean I'm *incapable* of functional relationships.

Right?

Maybe Tanya wasn't totally wrong about everything, whispers a nasty voice in the back of my mind. *Maybe you really are stupid, unlovable, unworthy . . .*

I hurriedly try to quash the memories of her cruel accusations. It's been a long time, and I can't let myself backslide to that dark place Tanya put me in. I can't let her back into my head.

But I can't stop thinking either. I toss and turn all night, tangling the sheets into a snarled mess before I finally fall asleep a few hours before dawn.

♡

My ringtone wakes me. Part of me hopes it's Keaton, and the other part hopes it's anyone but her. I fumble for my phone on the nightstand and see it's Mom calling.

Huh? I check the time and realize I've slept much later than I thought.

I sit up and answer the phone. "Hi, Mom."

"Oh, honey, what's wrong?"

The immediate interrogation catches me off guard. "Uh . . . nothing."

"No, not nothing. I can hear it in your voice. Tell me why you sound so depressed."

I suppress a groan. "Mom, please. It's nothing. I just woke up."

"Are you sure? I'm always here to help if you need advice."

That's actually not a terrible idea, if I can censor the story enough. I really don't feel like spilling all the dirty details of our hookups to my mother.

I release a heavy sigh and swing my legs over the side of the bed. Groggily, I stand and head to the kitchen toward my coffee maker. "Well . . . I have this friend. Who's a girl."

"Ohhh," Mom says, as if she already understands everything.

"We . . . hung out a lot." *Fucked like rabbits.* "And eventually, I realized I was developing feelings for her. So last night, I told her how I felt, and she said, 'No, you don't.'"

"You mean she didn't want to date you?"

"No. She said I didn't have feelings for her."

"What?" Mom sounds three parts bewildered and one part pissed off. At least I'm not the only one who's confused here.

"Yeah, I don't get it either." I sigh. "What the hell is wrong with me that she wouldn't even believe I'm capable of real feelings." I grab a mug from the cupboard and lean against the counter as I wait for my coffee to brew.

"Nothing is wrong with you, honey. The Lord just works in mysterious ways. When we lost your father . . ." Mom sighs into the receiver with a rush of static. "I've never seen such a terrible blizzard before or since. Ten-car pileup, and he was the only one who didn't walk away. I don't know why God chose him, but—"

"I remember it fine, Mom," I say, more tersely than I intended. "I was in high school, not preschool." And I'm really not in the mood to hear this story for the millionth time.

"There's no need for that tone."

"Sorry. I didn't mean to snap . . . just didn't sleep well."

And it's the truth. Even though her fate-and-destiny tangents annoy me sometimes, I get it—Mom had her way of moving on from Dad's death and I had mine.

"I'm just . . ." I heave a frustrated sigh. "I thought I'd figured out how to deal with that. I thought the lesson I had to learn was that I should live my life to the fullest, because nobody ever knows when it'll end, and once I accepted that, everything would work out. But now I don't have a clue anymore. Following my gut last night just ended up screwing me over."

She clucks in sympathy. "For what it's worth, honey, even though it didn't turn out how you'd hoped, I still think you did the right thing. Telling someone you love them is never a mistake."

"Then why do I feel so awful?" I mutter.

"Because you did something brave and honest and kind, and that girl threw it back in your face." I can practically see my mother pacing around her antique-crowded living room in agitation. "I'm just saying, this could be a sign she isn't good enough for you."

"Calm down, Mom. Remember your blood pressure. You don't have to get so worked up for me."

I don't have it in me to defend Keaton right now, but I don't need Mom taking sides either. I'm a grown-ass man who can fight his own battles. And also . . . deep down, despite my bruised heart, some part of me still doesn't want to hear anyone trash-talk Keaton.

"The hell I don't. I'm your mother, for heaven's sake. If this is Tanya all over aga—"

"No, it isn't. She's not like that." I'm surprised by the forcefulness in my own voice.

"All right, all right. I'm sure she was just confused and surprised, but it still wasn't a nice thing to say. Maybe she'll come to her senses and apologize, and maybe she won't. Right now, what's important is taking care of yourself. Get your rest, get something to eat, focus on taking care of yourself, and don't talk to her until you're ready to talk . . . or until she's ready to apologize."

That gets a halfhearted snort out of me. Of course she's telling me to eat. Doctor Mom, prescribing food for everything from headache to heartache. Then again, a microwave burrito can hardly make this situation any worse.

"I think I'm done sleeping for today. But thanks, Mom. I'll do the other two things."

"Good boy. I love you." A long pause. "Do you

still love her?"

"I think so. I just don't know if I . . ." Can ever touch her again. Open up to her again. Maybe even be friends with her again. God, what the fuck is going to happen to us? "I don't know if I should."

"I understand. Things are hard now, but you'll figure it out," Mom says with a confidence I wish I shared.

"I hope you're right," I say, pouring coffee into my mug.

"Of course I am. I'm a mom. Knowing everything is my job." She laughs at her own joke.

I chuckle despite myself, but I still want to change the subject. "Anyway, what've you been up to?"

I put her on speakerphone so I can heat up a frozen breakfast burrito and eat it while listening to her chatter merrily about the goings-on of her friends, her favorite shows, the neighborhood, the fabric store where she works part-time.

By the time my plate is empty and we've said our good-byes, I still feel hollow and broken, but maybe a little bit less awful than before Mom called. So maybe her predictions about the other stuff will come true too.

CHAPTER
Eighteen

Keaton

S LATE DOESN'T LOVE ME. THIS IS THE THOUGHT that threatens to spill out of my mouth every time it passes through my mind.

I'm busier than I've ever been. It's the last day of our fiscal quarter, and I'm in the office on a Sunday morning, trying to wrap everything up. I'm juggling multiple phone calls with clients and distributors, but the conversation from last night won't leave me alone long enough to focus on the work at hand. I find myself repeating in my mind how much Slate is truly and deeply *not* in love with me, despite what he may say or think.

There's no way that's even remotely possible. This isn't some cheesy rom-com flick where the sweet, nerdy girl changes the playboy. This is my life. I promised myself I wouldn't confuse our physical acts with something emotional, and I haven't.

I don't think? But now Slate has, and it's upended everything.

I really want to talk to someone, anyone, about this. My first impulse is to reach out to Karina. She'd confirm my doubts about Slate's confession in a heartbeat. She knows Slate almost as well as I do.

Slate is too immature for a serious relationship, Keaton, she would say. *He may think he loves you, but it's more likely that he just realized he actually enjoys having sex with someone he cares about rather than blindly fucking around with random strangers he picks up in a bar.*

Karina's voice in my head sounds a little too much like my own. I honestly don't know what she would say about Slate's feelings. She doesn't know the whole story. The mind-blowing sex, the secret glances, the soft kisses, the indescribable embraces . . .

All Karina knows is that Slate planned a memorial service for my dead cat. That must have seemed very out of character. Slate can't even manage his own personal daily routine, let alone put together an event that involves sensitivity, punctuality, and creativity. He proved us all wrong.

He proved more than his organizational skills, I can hear Karina say. *He proved he cares about you. A lot.*

And maybe he does care about me. But love? I didn't think love was in Slate's vocabulary. At least, it hasn't been since that shitstorm with Tanya.

I hang up the phone after a particularly difficult sales call. Leaning back in my chair, I push my hands into my hair and sigh.

Logically, Slate and I don't make any sense. He's the kind of guy who drives to the airport with no plan in mind and takes the cheapest one-way flight to God knows where—*just for fun*. I'm the kind of woman who does her neighbor's taxes just for fun. There's an obvious difference between being sexually compatible with someone and romantically compatible. While the former is definitely a ten out of ten in my book, the latter is too risky to consider.

And yet, as I chew on the end of my pen, I'm considering it. The look in his eyes when he said he loved me was just so . . .

No. If Slate loved me, *really* loved me, and if—God forbid—I loved him back, that could seriously fuck up everything good about our friendship. There could be bickering and jealousy, and a total disregard for boundaries. All of that becomes way too complicated with love on the table. Best to go back to the basics and start from scratch, like a brand-new budget at the start of the quarter.

I pull up a fresh spreadsheet and stare at the empty cells. My mind is equally blank. I have zero motivation, and my pen is nearly chewed through.

Okay, new tactic.

I pull out my phone and scroll through past texts between Slate and me. How do we usually talk? Over the past few weeks, our conversations have been littered with sexual innuendos and embarrassing emoji-speak. Time to go further back.

My thumb pauses its scrolling on the day before he texted me after the disastrous bachelorette party, aka the first milestone of this downward spiral. The thread begins with a message from him.

Hey! How was your day?

> Meh, same old, same old. I'm
> hungry.

Perfect. Want to grab something to eat?

> No big date plans for tonight?
> I'm shocked.

Just me, you, and some juicy burgers.

Oh my God, I'm there.

The conversation is simple, short, and pleasant. *Perfect.* I begin drafting a new text to Slate. Why reinvent the wheel?

Hey! How's your day?

Now I sit back and wait. He's probably upset still, so it may take him a bit to—

Buzz!

I wasn't expecting such an immediate response.

Fine.

Wow. That single word has more subtext than any message I've ever sent or received.

Just fine?

Yeah, that about covers it.

Is he angry with me? Or is he sad? My heart weighs heavy at the likelihood of it being a messy concoction of both.

```
One more question. Are WE fine?
```

This time there's a long wait. I pick out a new pen to start destroying.

```
                    Yeah, Keaton, we're fine.
```

Why don't I believe you? I so badly want to ask him this. That isn't fair, though. I should just leave him alone. That's what he wants, isn't it?

Fuck it.

```
Obviously, we aren't fine. I'm
coming over.
```

Classic me, digging myself into a deeper and deeper hole.

I pick up my bag and coat, my heart pounding, and head straight for the elevator. I won't let things fizzle out like this. My friendship with Slate is way too important. I refuse to accept a reality in which our bond is at all altered from what it's always been.

On the Uber ride over to his place, I gnaw on my fingernails and practice my friendship speech.

Slate, I really think that we just need to take a moment to appreciate how amazing our friendship is.

The fact that we could have easy, meaningless sex and can still shoot the shit and be supportive adults to each other is amazing. We don't need to lose any of that. We can't lose that. You can't—

The car pulls up to the curb and I climb out.

My racing mind screeches to a cartoon-cliff halt when I stand at his door, my fist hovering inches from the dark wood. *What if he doesn't want to see me? What if I only make it worse?*

I knock.

And knock again.

No response. I can't help but feel like I've really, really fucked up.

Just as I'm about to give up, I hear the soft shuffle of feet on the other side of the door. I swallow. The door opens.

I barely recognize the man in front of me. Slate, always a figure of masculine hygiene and personal style, is a complete mess. He's wearing the same loungewear I've seen him in a thousand times, but his defeated posture somehow makes it look worn and shabby. His face is unshaven, and his usually vibrant eyes lack that sparkle I've come to expect. This isn't the man I know.

"Hey," he mutters, propping the door open. He tilts his head in a reluctant invitation into his apartment. I take a cautious step in, realizing only now how inappropriate it was for me to just show up like this.

"I'm sorry for forcing you to see me," I blurt, half apologizing, half hopeful that he'll assure me that no apology is necessary. *Like the old Slate would.*

"It's fine."

I can feel tears forming. I've never hated the word *fine* more.

"We're still friends, right?" I ask, unable to mask the desperation in my voice.

We're standing just beyond the threshold of his door. My throat is tight and my chest is burning. To any onlooker, the awkward distance between us would make us look like complete strangers. I try not to dwell on that.

Why is it taking him so fucking long to answer? My stomach drops to my feet.

"Slate?"

"Yeah. Yeah, Keaton." He sighs and reaches out, and I eagerly grab his hand in an effort to close this gaping hole between us. "We're still friends."

I savor the warmth of his fingers in mine. The tightness in my throat constricts until he continues.

"We're still friends . . . but I can't have sex with you anymore." Long, awkward pause. "You've graduated, anyway. You're the master now." He says this last part with a forced smile.

"The apprentice always outdoes the master at some point." I hear the levity of my words, but I don't feel any lighter. I feel like a fraud.

"That's what they say."

We stand like that, our hands limply attached for another moment. I can't bear it any longer.

"I'd better head out. Thanks for . . ." I honestly don't know how to continue. "Everything."

"Sure." He opens the door for me. "'Bye, Keat."

"'Bye, Slate."

♡

Back in the office, the void in my stomach has nothing to do with skipping lunch. Things will be fine. I've had bouts of petty miscommunication and even a little heartache with Gabby and Karina before. We'd give each other the space we needed, and then bounce back to normal within a few days.

But Slate isn't like my other friends, I realize. The situation with him is so obviously different. We crossed out of friend territory and wandered naively into a gray area. A strikingly beautiful, tragically dangerous gray area. Then I let go and backtracked, leaving him to wander the gray alone. I left him there, all because I'm too scared to—

"Hey, Keaton."

I jolt at the sound of a man's baritone voice. When I look up, a newly chewed pen falls gracelessly from my lips and onto my desk with a sharp clatter. "Oh, hey, Jerome."

The office hunk stands with one hand casually propping him against my desk.

How did I not hear him approach? Usually my Jerome sensors are fine-tuned to the sound of his footsteps and the scent of his unobtrusive cologne.

"You really did a number on that pen," he says with a friendly smile. His teeth sparkle in the fluorescent lights of the office.

I wipe my mouth with the back of my hand. "Yeah, well," I say, no clue where I'm heading, "it's early afternoon and I'm already daydreaming about what I'm going to eat for dinner." *What the fuck, Keaton?*

"What do you want?" he asks, genuinely interested.

"There's this Thai restaurant I've been dying to go to." *With Slate.*

"Oh man, I haven't had Thai food in a while. Mind if I join you?"

My heart stops. Is the office heartthrob really

asking me out? Or is he just in it for the Thai? I've told Karina and Gabby that he's cute, and he is—in a textbook kind of way, and I know a lot of the women I work with think he's hot. But honestly? He's never really done it for me.

"You can say no," he says reassuringly. "I realize I'm intruding on your daydreams."

No, really, you aren't, I want to say. I've been day-dreaming about you every day since . . . My thoughts pause. I really haven't been daydreaming about Jerome anymore, have I?

"Thai food with a side of company. Sure. Sounds great."

♡

"Who is Jerome? What about that other nice man?" Meera asks me for the third time since I crash-land-ed at her kitchen table. I only have a half hour before Jerome picks me up and we head to the restaurant.

In my panic, I knocked on Meera's door, know-ing there was no Penny behind my own to absorb my raging emotions. Always welcoming to compa-ny, Meera led me inside and sat me down at the ta-ble with a hot cup of tea. I sip on it, the subtle spic-es doing absolutely nothing to calm my fluttering *everything.*

"He's the man I'm supposed to have dinner with in under an hour!" I squeak, answering her question. "But I promised Slate a while back that we'd go to this restaurant together. Slate loves Thai food, and it would be an absolute betrayal of our friendship if I went with some random guy from work!" I pick anxiously at the tablecloth. "I should be so excited for this! He's a huge catch. He actually runs marathons for charity. Like, who does that?"

Meera ignores anything I say about Jerome, waving the words away like pesky flies. "You feel you would betray Slate if you went to dinner with another man?"

I take an audible gulp of my tea before unequivocally answering, "Yes."

"And Slate is just your friend?" she asks.

"Slate is more than a friend!" I hear myself saying. *Uh-oh.*

Meera sits back and smiles.

Goddammit.

"It sounds like you have love for Slate."

"It isn't like that. He's just my friend, one of my best friends, actually. At least, he was—"

"Love is friendship, but it is friendship with fire in its belly."

The words of this wise woman poke at my

furiously beating heart. My cheeks turn warmer and warmer.

I don't want to admit it, but I know she's right. I know the truth. It's in the thumping of my heart, the shortness of my breath, the coiling knot of my stomach. The way I've been shouting everything at her for the past fifteen minutes. My dread at the thought of going out with Jerome. The devastation I felt when I saw Slate looking so broken today.

I know what I have to do. First, I need to call Jerome and cancel. The rest of it will be a lot more complicated.

CHAPTER
Nineteen

Slate

OR A LONG TIME AFTER I WAKE UP SATURDAY morning, I just lie in bed, staring at the ceiling, in no hurry to get up. I made it through the work week somehow, but the loss I feel over my connection with Keaton has left a black hole inside my chest.

I'm never going to get over her, and going back to being just friends isn't something I'm ready to think about. I have no idea how I can go out to brunch with her now, and sit across the table from her while pretending everything is fine.

The truth is, I'm deeply in love with her. Yeah, maybe it took this little experiment of hers to push me in this direction, but now that I know her on this whole new level, it's obvious. She's the total package. And the thought of her with another guy sends stabbing pains straight through my heart.

A loud knock pulls me out of my dark thoughts. With an annoyed grunt, I roll out of bed and trudge to the door. I probably look as shitty as I feel, but that's the last thing I'm concerned with. I feel as if I've been wrung out and fed through a shredder.

When I open the door, the last person I expect to find is Keaton. But she's standing here, and I have to physically steady myself by pressing one hand against the door frame.

She's dressed casually in a red cardigan, dark jeans, and heeled boots. She looks amazing, as always. Her clothes hug her curves so enticingly, and whatever she's done with her makeup emphasizes her full lips and deep blue eyes. I wish I didn't ache to touch her. I wish she wasn't here, and yet I wish she'd never leave.

"Hi, Slate," she says. "How's it hanging?"

A million thoughts jostle to be spoken. *This is killing me. I love you. I'm so confused all the time. I'm pissed at you and pissed at myself, but I still would've cleaned up if I'd known you were coming, because I'm a pathetic dumbass. Just leave me alone. I want to kiss you, hold you, hear you say . . .*

But all that falls out of my mouth is a flat, "Oh. Hey. Did you, uh, forget something here?" That's just what I need to put the last nail in my coffin, finding a random pair of her panties in my bed.

"I did. You." She pokes me in the chest. "Get dressed. I have a surprise for you." She pushes past me before I can react.

I blink at her retreating back as she bustles into my bedroom, then follow her. "Huh?"

"Hurry up. Our flight leaves in two hours." She drags my overnight bag out of my closet and starts tossing T-shirts and socks into it.

What the hell?

"Flight? What on earth are you talking about?"

Still flinging my clothes around like a tornado, she looks back at me with an excited, almost mischievous smirk. "I know you passed up your favorite team's big game for Penny's wake. So I bought us two tickets."

"But . . . what?" My brain feels like it's grinding to keep up with all the information she's throwing at me. "They aren't playing anywhere near here for months."

"I know. That's why we're flying to Chicago. I booked us a hotel room for the night too. I thought we could hit some bars after the game, have some fun."

"Why are you doing this?"

My words halt her in her tracks. Keaton drops

her gaze for a second, looking sheepish, then meets my eyes again. "I shouldn't have said all that stuff last weekend. I acted really mean and inappropriate. I'm sorry. I wanted to make it up to you . . . and, to be honest, I also just wanted to see you. I've missed you."

It's only an apology for the *way* she rejected me, not actually *taking back* her rejection. Definitely not an *I love you too*.

But I'm still touched that she's going to all this effort to repair our friendship. And I have to admit, the prospect of seeing my favorite basketball team play and hanging out with Keaton sounds great. Just like old times.

The shitty mood that's been weighing me down for the past week is already starting to turn around. This, I decide, is an olive branch I'm more than willing to accept.

"It's okay." I crack a smile.

Her eyes soften in affection and relief as she smiles back. "No, it wasn't. But thanks for saying so. Now, hurry up and get dressed."

I raise my eyebrows at her. "You have to get out of my bedroom first."

"Oh. Right. Excuse me." With a lopsided grin, she slips out.

Keaton does realize we can't see each other naked anymore, right? As much as that truth hurts, this is our new normal now, and it really and truly sucks.

Trying not to think about all that right now, I throw on a pair of dark jeans, a light blue polo, and my most comfortable shoes. Then I head into the bathroom where I wash my face, brush and floss my teeth, and quickly work some styling product into my hair. Once I finish packing, I rejoin Keaton in the living room.

Within fifteen minutes, we're speeding down the highway to the airport. Even though I know it might not be wise for my heart to spend the night with her, I want nothing more. I'm starting to appreciate that any Keaton is better than no Keaton at all.

♡

Our plane lands with just enough time for us to catch a taxi to the stadium and find our seats before the afternoon game starts. We each get a cold beer and share a tub of popcorn.

In the end, the Bulls squeak through with a narrow victory, but nothing can sour the fun of sitting next to my best friend, booing good-naturedly, watching my favorite team make one of their biggest rivals fight for every inch.

For dinner, we visit a restaurant that Keaton claims has incredible deep-dish pizza, according to her internet research. Her prediction comes true. Between us, we make a sizable dent in a large pie and enjoy a couple of beers.

"Holy crap, it's hot in here." She unbuttons her cardigan, then wriggles out of it to reveal the low-cut tank top underneath, and hangs her sweater on the back of her chair. "You having fun?"

Yeah, almost too much. I take a long drink of my beer to avoid staring at her cleavage. "Are you kidding? This has been pretty much the best night ever. How long did it even take you to organize everything?"

"Pretty much all week. That's why I fell off the face of the earth, because I wasn't sure it was going to happen." She pokes out the tip of her tongue, grinning impishly. "But don't worry, handsome, I'm all yours tonight."

I almost choke on my beer. "Wh-what?" I must have misheard or misunderstood or *something*, because . . .

"You have my undivided attention. For all of dinner, drinks . . . and whatever you want to come after drinks." Holding my gaze with hers, she gives me a smile full of unmistakable promise.

My mouth dries up. Keaton is definitely flirting with me. Or am I trying to make this more than what it really is? What the hell is going on here? I thought we were done with that part of our relationship. But her signals couldn't be clearer. And now she's watching to see how I'll react, running her fingertip around the rim of her glass.

Somehow the implications of what she said earlier didn't hit me until now. She booked us a hotel room . . . as in, singular. Possibly even one bed. But she doesn't want that, right?

Really, I have no idea what's going to happen back at the hotel tonight. I'm not even sure what I hope will happen. I want her, of course, want her desperately, but sex would be a terrible idea. We just broke up—not even broke up, because we were never really "together" in the first place. Keaton made her feelings pretty damn clear last weekend.

So, why is she practically yelling FUCK ME into a megaphone? She never does anything without a well-thought-out reason . . . after weighing every pro and con.

Still, despite my confusion, it's hard not to be flattered by the attention. I smirk at her. "Whatever I want, huh? I'll hold you to that."

She looks pleased, a little relieved . . . and also

very interested. "I hope so."

After I insist on paying the bill, we walk a few blocks to a nearby bar, another place Keaton scoped out in advance. The sidewalk has more than enough space, but she sticks so close to me that our arms brush together.

Should I hold her hand? I decide not to. I still have no idea what I should do, what she's aiming for, what touching her would mean. I can't set myself up for more rejection. Mixed signals are firing off like rockets all around us right now, fucking with my mind.

She stops us at a bar that's small, but busy. It's unpretentious, clean, and quietly classy, with yellowed lighting, worn hardwood floors, and only a few tables, all full. We sit at the polished counter and order our usual. As I sip my vodka soda, the questions crowding the back of my mind grow too big to ignore any longer.

Tonight's been a blast; I almost don't want to risk ruining this perfect evening by bringing up any tough questions. But we need to hash this out. I need to make sure I understand everything crystal clear, with no vagueness or miscommunication. And I need to ask before we order any more drinks and alcohol starts to color our decisions. I need answers before we cross the threshold of our hotel room door.

"So . . ." My tone must tip her off, because Keaton sets down her drink and looks at me.

"Yeah?"

"What . . ." *God, how do I say this?* "What are we doing here?"

She bats her eyes at me. "For starters, handsome, I'm buying us another round."

There's that *handsome* again. What the hell is with that? "You know what I mean. Where do we stand?"

Keaton steeples her fingers in front of her mouth, then lets out a pensive sigh. "A very wise woman told me 'love is just friendship, but it is friendship with fire in its belly,' and I realized she was right. I've been way overthinking the line we drew between lovers and friends. I thought the two things were totally different, when really . . ." She looks at me, and I could drown in the deep blue of her eyes. "It's so easy for one to evolve into the other."

Is she going where I think she's going with this? I hardly dare to let myself believe it. I definitely don't dare to interrupt her in case she clams up.

"I'm sorry for the way I shot you down. I want to try again. For real this time. Me and you . . . seeing where it goes." She hesitates. "If you still want me."

For a minute, I just stare at Keaton. I must be hearing things . . . but I'm not. She really wants to be with me, the way I want to be with her.

Swallowing hard, I take a deep breath. "You mean, you want us to be together? As in more than just friends? As in you've graduated from Sexploration 101 and we're now moving on to Relationships 201?"

She nods, her mouth tilting up in a smile. Then she gives me a grin that warms me from the inside out. "I miss us. And the naked stuff too. A lot."

I take her hand. "Then let's pay our tab and get the hell out of here."

Keaton giggles, and that sound is the best thing I've ever heard.

The taxi back to our hotel can't drive fast enough.

♡

We're barely through the door before Keaton crashes into my arms. I meet her kiss with equal hunger, and a loud groan escapes me when her tongue caresses mine.

God, this feels so right. I didn't realize just how badly I'd missed being able to touch her. How could I ever bear to stay away?

I reach under her sweater to squeeze her breasts through her bra, savoring their plush softness. She moans and presses against me, making it clear she's ready for more.

"Tell me how you want it, baby." The endearment slips out. But we're lovers now, I'm allowed to say things like that, and her answering smile chases away whatever doubts and fears may have lingered.

"There *is* something I wanted to try . . . one last lesson we never got to before. You taking me from behind."

Just the words make my cock twitch. "That's right. We never got our special night at the hotel, did we? Well, if we're going to do that, I want to give you everything I had planned."

In the bedroom, we undress each other as fast as we can; my hands are almost shaking with anticipation at the feel of her silky skin. It's so tempting to just take her right then and there, but I know from experience this will be even better if we savor it, let our desires build.

"Lie on the bed," I murmur. "I'll be right there."

I find some scented lotion in the bathroom and come back. For a moment, I pause in the doorway to drink in the sight of her . . . bare, waiting, all laid out for me on her stomach. Then I straddle her ass, smooth lotion over her back, and start massaging her shoulders. They're knotted with tension, likely from sitting at a computer desk all week. The way she moans and gasps with relief tempts me again, but I force myself to work slowly, thoroughly, all the way down her back.

After a few minutes, she mumbles something into the pillow.

"What's that?" I ask.

She sighs. "I never should have turned you down last weekend."

Where did that come from? "You already apologized for that."

"I was being so stupid . . . I was convinced we'd never work as anything more than friends. I told myself we were too different, you didn't really feel anything for me, you couldn't possibly adjust to being a one-woman man—whatever bullshit excuse I could come up with, just because I was scared of getting hurt. I said all those things when all along I knew you were someone I couldn't bear to ever let go."

I'm floored. I can't think of any response, so I just lean down and kiss her cheek, hoping that will say enough. She twists her head to meet my lips with hers.

"God, when I think I almost missed my chance with you," she murmurs. "I'm such a fucking idiot. Isn't it ridiculous, a grown-ass woman who couldn't handle a leap of faith?"

"It's okay, Keat. We're starting over." I run one finger down the graceful dip of her spine. "And just so you know, for you, I can absolutely be a one-woman man."

She sighs happily. I reach under her body to cup and squeeze her breasts. Her breathing hitches. I gently pinch her nipples and she arches, pushing her hips up, offering herself. I press flush against her back to kiss the nape of her neck and grind my aching cock against her ass. She squirms helplessly against me.

Finally, when neither of us can take another second of teasing, I grab a condom from the nightstand and roll it on. I push inside her, and she moans softly. I don't stop until I'm buried inside her warmth as far as I'll go.

"You all right?" I ask, my voice gruff.

"Yeah, it just . . . wow." Her voice is already rough and breathy. "You're so deep."

I smirk. "I know. And you feel fucking incredible."

"So good," she mumbles.

I slide my fingers down between her thighs. She's soaking wet, her clit like a hard slick pearl, and just the lightest brush makes her gasp. I start thrusting while rubbing her, careful to keep the angle that makes her cry out with every slow pump of my hips.

Her hands are white-knuckled, knotted in the sheets. I wish I could see her face, but she's mine now—I know we'll have many more times to come, many more chances to see her dissolve in bliss, and nothing could make me happier. Besides, I certainly can't complain about the view of her round hips, her shapely ass, and her silky hair cascading over the pillow.

She's started trembling, panting, her moans louder and more urgent. I work my fingers faster between her thighs, desperate to make her come. She turns to look back at me over her shoulder.

"Oh, Slate . . . oh!" Her half-lidded eyes, dark with desire, transfix me.

Recalling another of the items on her spreadsheet, I stroke one finger between her cheeks, eliciting a pleasure-filled sound I've never heard her make before.

"You're so fucking sexy, Keat." I close my eyes for a moment, moaning through gritted teeth. She's going to make me lose control much faster than I wanted. But it's been too long, and having her again is like a monsoon after a drought. It's too much. Too intense.

"I can't wait to take you here, baby," I murmur,

still stroking her sexy backside, and lean close to press my lips to the back of her neck.

Then her eyes flutter closed, her mouth falls slack, and I can feel her orgasm hit her in waves, clenching around my cock from the inside and spasming against my fingers from the outside. Overwhelmed, moaning aloud, I tumble over the edge after her.

With pleasure-weakened arms, I gather her close to my chest. She drapes herself over me—I couldn't ask for a better blanket—and soon her breathing slows. Just when I think she's fallen asleep, she pulls back slightly, looking into my eyes.

Almost tentatively, she says, "I love you."

I pour every ounce of the tender fire I feel for her into my kiss. "I love you too."

This is us . . . starting over. And it's been the perfect night.

Entwined, we fall asleep together, and spend the night secure in each other's arms.

CHAPTER
Twenty

Keaton

B Y SOME MIRACLE, SLATE AND I MAKE IT TO THE group brunch without tearing each other's clothes off again. Even more improbable is the fact that we arrive before Karina and Gabby.

As we enter the diner, I rake my fingers through my sex hair in an attempt to tame it. After the third impossible knot, I give up. I can't hide the evidence of how I spent my morning. I wish I was twenty again, when putting my hair up in a messy bun was still public appropriate.

Fuck it. Up it goes.

"I thought for sure we were going to be late." I pile my hair on my head without the help of a mirror to guide me, hoping I look presentable. But that's the best part about my new relationship with Slate. He knows me. He's seen me at my worst. And still, he loves me.

Our usual booth by the far window is open, and Slate's fingertips at my lower back guide me toward the rear of the diner. I wiggle my way down the bench until I'm cozy.

"Rolling you out of bed wasn't easy." The cushion gives as Slate scoots in next to me.

I examine my reflection in the glass of the diner window. *It could be worse.* "Oh, please. It was all 'five more minutes, please' and morning wood from you," I scoff.

"Because you clearly *hated* where that led us, Miss Bedhead."

I turn back to him with a smirk, armed and ready with a comment about his own mess of hair and ready to fire, until—"Wait."

"What?" He smiles, certain he's won this round.

"You *never* sit by me."

He blinks. "What do you mean?"

"On the bench. You always sit across from me, in the chair." I point for emphasis.

"So?" The corner of his mouth quirks upward, a typical sign of Slate not taking me seriously.

The waitress drops by our table, leaving four glasses of ice water with the promise to be back in just a second.

"Gabby and Karina are going to be here any

minute. They'll notice if we're sitting in different spots. It'll look like . . ."

Oh. Only now am I realizing how silly I sound.

"Like we're together?" He leans closer and kisses me sweetly on the cheek. "They're going to figure it out regardless. Hell, they probably already know. We weren't exactly being inconspicuous at the club." His voice drops to a sexy growl as he skims a hand up my thigh.

I swat it away as if to scold him. "That was totally your fault." After the words leave my mouth, I realize I sound ten years younger than I am.

Slate stares at my lips as I speak, then he touches my thigh again with even more enthusiasm, giving it a good, hard squeeze under the table. I clutch his hand as he slides it to my knee.

"You're incredibly frustrating," he murmurs, his mouth close to my neck.

I place one hand over the front of his jeans, teasing him. "And you're not? Besides, you're incredibly hard."

Karina is suddenly at the end of the table, with one perfectly shaped eyebrow raised. She *must* have seen all of that grabbing in high definition.

Gabby, meanwhile, slumps into her usual spot across from me. She wears a grimace and a pair of chic hangover shades to top off her trademark morning-after look.

"Hey!" I squeak. My hands fly up to the table and *not anywhere near* my best friend's penis.

"You two both look like you've run a marathon," Karina says as she takes the seat across from Slate. The new arrangement definitely doesn't escape her. She looks around, taking in the landscape with an amused smile.

"Something like that," Slate says, and I want to pinch him.

"Hmm." Karina sounds unconvinced. If she didn't know before, she definitely knows now.

Chill out, Keaton. Why are you so nervous?

Maybe it's because Slate and I haven't decided when or how we'll tell them. About us. God, I still can't believe there is an *us*.

I clear my throat. "What took you guys so long?"

"Traffic, her hangover, et cetera," Karina replies, rubbing sympathetic circles on poor Gabby's back.

Gabby lowers her sunglasses, looking over them. "I may be dying, but at least I lived," she shoots back with a sly wink.

Karina swiftly directs the conversation back on track. "So, anything new with you two?"

Does our groundbreaking, life-changing love story count?

With perfect timing, the waitress materializes at the end of our booth to take our orders. It's burritos for Slate and me, apple-cinnamon waffles and black coffee for Gabby, and biscuits and gravy with a side of fruit for Karina.

Meanwhile, my thoughts are racing.

Why am I being like this? I'm neither embarrassed by my feelings for Slate, nor do I want to keep them a secret from Gabby or Karina any longer. So, why is it so hard to just say it? *We're more than friends.* I try the words out behind closed lips but find myself swallowing them along with all my anxieties.

I imagine their wide eyes and worried tones . . .

Never date your friends! What if this makes it weird? What if you two fight or break up, and we have to pick sides? What does that mean for all of us? Have you two thought this through? What if it doesn't work out and you two ruin the friendship you have? What if you ruin the friendship we all have?

These are questions I have, myself. And I hate that I don't have the answers yet.

Under the table, a firm hand grips mine. I look at Slate. There are questions in his eyes too. But there's a confidence in that classic sparkle of his gaze.

Comforted by the warmth of his hand and the

clarity in his eyes, I feel my anxieties start to fade away. Slate is right here too. We're together in this moment and the next. Everything will be okay.

"I'm going to say this now," Slate says in earnest, "so no one throws up their brunch."

"Okay?" Karina raises her eyebrows again in concern.

"I may lose those waffles regardless of what you say," Gabby says with a quiet sigh.

Slate looks at me with a smile. I smile back. This is good. Then Slate says my new favorite combination of words.

"Keaton and I—we're together now."

These words fill me with an inexplicable joy. I would kiss him right now if I weren't so preoccupied with the looks on our friends' faces. Their blank expressions are giving absolutely nothing away.

We all sit in silence as the waitress pours us each a cup of coffee. The sound of each pour is a little more unbearable than the last. Finally, the waitress leaves us.

"Well?" I say, urging someone to say something.

Suddenly, Gabby crumples into heaving laughter.

Slate and I exchange a look. *Of course.*

"I thought you two had killed someone and wanted us to hide a damn body or something! You were so pale!" Gabby is almost in tears. "Oh my God, this is so good . . ."

Karina takes a sip of fresh coffee, her matte lipstick not leaving a trace on the ceramic edge. "I mean, I'm a little offended that you thought we'd be shocked, like this was actual news or something. It's been so obvious."

"Really?" I ask, baffled. Next to me, Slate runs a hand down my spine with a soft chuckle.

"Yeah, girl," Gabby says. "Man, this is awkward. For you, I mean."

"Thank you, Gabby," I say through gritted teeth. I can't figure out the look on Karina's face.

"Can someone pass the sugar? I just can't do black coffee like Mateo can." She shakes her head in mild disgust.

My God, what is with these two? I want to shake them by their shoulders and bear-hug them at the same time.

Slate secures a handful of sugar packets for his own coffee before handing her the caddy.

"How long have you known?" I ask, wondering where we slipped our secret.

"I've known since the cat funeral." Gabby picks up her glass of water and takes a slow sip. "Who plans a funeral for a cat? Slate was so obviously in love with you. Like disgusting in love, wants-to-father-your-child in love."

"Okay now . . ." Slate leans forward to steal Gabby's sunglasses, but she shrugs him out of the way. "You aren't wrong," he says, smiling.

My stomach does another flip.

"The cat funeral was really strange . . . and really damn cute." Karina smiles warmly at me, with a look in her eye that says, *You really thought you could hide this from me?* "But, honestly, you guys are perfect together. I'm just glad you finally figured that out."

Feeling sheepish, I smile back, a blush and a nod serving as the best apology I can offer.

Slate touches my cheek, his warm palm turning my face toward his. And then his lips press against mine in a sweet, brief kiss. "Love you, Keat."

My heart swells in my chest, and I feel better than I have in years—or maybe ever. "I love you too."

I expect some comment about how gross we are, or that public displays of affection won't be tolerated, but instead I find Karina and Gabby grinning at us.

"You guys are too damn cute."

The waitress returns shortly after with our meals. The four of us dig in, our laughter filling the diner and my heart with joy.

CHAPTER
Twenty-One

Slate

"Baby, I'm home," I call, shutting our front door behind me with one foot. My hands are occupied with a plastic animal carrier and a shopping bag full of pet supplies. "And I've got a surprise for you."

Keaton's standing on tiptoe, her back to me, rummaging through the top shelf of a kitchen cabinet. "I hope it's pizza, because I think I forgot to buy beef broth for the dinner tonight."

I grin. She looks so cute in sweatpants and a messy ponytail.

It's been two months since we moved in together, six months since we became "official," and I'm still not over the pleasure of being able to see her all the time, so casual and domestic.

"Nope. Something better than pizza."

Keaton turns around. I hold up the pet carrier so

she can see through the wire door to what's curled up inside—a fluffy orange tabby kitten with emerald-green eyes.

Keaton's blue eyes blink, then go wide. "Oh my God . . . she's adorable. Or is it a he?"

"She's a she." I set down the carrier in the middle of the living room and open the door.

Keaton kneels about a foot away, careful not to crowd our tiny guest. "Hey there, baby girl, it's nice to meet you," she murmurs, keeping her voice soft and sweet.

The kitten creeps to the lip of the carrier, peers around for a minute, then steps out onto the carpet. Slowly, Keaton holds out her hand. The kitten sniffs it thoroughly. Then, as if she's come to a decision, she bumps her head against Keaton's fingers.

Biting back a squeal, Keaton pets her. "She likes me!"

I chuckle. "Of course. I think you're pretty likable."

"Aw, thank you, sweetie. But you have to say that—you're my boyfriend, and you like a lot of sex." She leans closer and the kitten bats at the tip of her dangling ponytail.

I peck Keaton on the forehead. "Just because I have to say it doesn't mean it's not true . . . but you're right about the sex. I'll never get tired of fucking you, baby."

Keaton waggles her fingers until the kitten snatches at them, her claws out and pupils huge. "How old is she? Does she have all her shots? What about a name?" she asks, rapid-fire.

"The rescue shelter figured she was about four months old. They handled shots and spaying too. They were calling her Beans, but I thought we could choose a new name together."

Keaton snorts. "Beans, really?"

"Apparently."

"Hmm . . ." She studies the kitten, who has now moved on to attacking her fingers with teeth too small to do any real damage. "Reminds me of another cat I used to know."

I'm glad to see her talking about Penny with a smile rather than tears. Ever since she died, it's been clear that Keaton has carried a cat-shaped hole in her heart. As much as I'd wanted to make a home for the both of us—and as far as Keaton's concerned, a house isn't a home without something furry climbing the curtains—I also didn't want to run out and buy a replacement Penny too soon. So I held off until today to make sure Keaton was ready to move on.

"If she really is Penny's spiritual successor, we

should find a name that starts with *P*." I sit down beside Keaton. "What about . . . Pancake? Or Prissy?"

Keaton playfully smacks me in the shoulder with the back of her hand. "No way."

I fake an innocently thoughtful look. "Poltergeist. Peaches. Porkchop. Pumpkin."

She laughs, shaking her head. "You're the worst." Then she rubs her chin, considering. "Actually . . . Peaches kinda works for me. Her fur looks like peaches and cream."

"Sold. Peaches, it is." I scratch our newly christened daughter under her fuzzy chin. Her whiskers flare out and her vivid eyes slide shut with pleasure. "Welcome to the family, Peaches."

Keaton rests her forehead on my shoulder with a happy sigh. "Thank you so much, Slate. This is . . . I love her."

I kiss the crown of her head. "And I love you."

We sit like that for a long time, Keaton's head on me, my arm around her waist, Peaches still playing with her fingers. It's nice being here with Keat, watching the clumsy little kitten explore.

After a few more minutes, I let out a sigh. "As much as I don't want to move, I have to go get her litter box out of the car. I couldn't carry everything in one trip."

Keaton reluctantly stands when I rise to my feet, and much less reluctantly kisses me. "I'll set up her other stuff."

When I return with the plastic tray and bag of litter, Keaton has put down the kitten's food and water bowls, filled both to the brim, and scattered the handful of toys over the living room floor. She's scribbling down notes about what else we need, muttering to herself.

"A small kitty bed . . . dental treats for your teeth . . . a scratching post, absolutely . . ." She looks down at Peaches, who's demolishing a hill of minced turkey in gravy. "Or maybe a full-size cat tree. What do you think, girl? Something to climb and wreck that's not the couch?"

Peaches meows, her response somewhat garbled by her full mouth.

I have to chuckle at the sight. All of it, from the meticulous planning to the conversing with cats, it's all just so Keaton. "About that pizza—you want our usual?"

Keaton gives me a grateful smile. "Yes, please. Thank you for rescuing us from my dinner mishap."

"Hey, I could've picked up that broth too. Don't worry about it. We're celebrating tonight . . . call it Peaches' welcome party."

I order a large barbecue chicken pizza from our favorite pizzeria. I'm just hanging up the phone when something thwaps the back of my calf. I look down to find Peaches clinging to my pant leg.

"You got bored with eating already?" I peel her off me, only for her to wriggle out of my grasp and dash away to explore the rest of the apartment. I shake my head, chuckling. "Didn't take long to start acting like she owns the place."

"Well, of course. That's what cats are for," Keaton calls from the laundry room where she's pouring litter into Peaches' tray.

After we eat, we snuggle together on the couch, happy and content. Peaches climbs up onto the armrest and tucks her paws underneath her so she looks like a tiny loaf of orange bread. The picture of a peaceful family is complete. Contentment radiates from us all, so warm and bright, I swear I must be glowing.

Keaton freezes, her head lifted partway from my shoulder where it has been resting. "Listen," she says, her voice hushed, almost awed.

At first, I have no idea what she means. Then I hear it. Peaches has started purring.

Keaton curls up against my side and kisses me. "This is everything I've ever wanted."

"Me too." I hold her tight, this amazing woman who went from my best friend to my lover to my partner . . . to my home.

It may have taken us a while to cross from the friend zone and into this new territory together, but it's been a seamless transition. And one exactly no one was surprised about—from our friends to our parents, and even our coworkers, who all met the news of our coupledom with bored noninterest, like something long overdue was finally happening. I guess the only ones who were surprised were Keaton and me.

After I clean up the kitchen by loading our plates into the dishwasher, I pour Keaton a glass of white wine and rejoin her on the couch. Rather than watching the comedy special we've selected, Keaton only has eyes for Peaches.

"Look," she whispers sweetly. "She's falling asleep."

The kitten's eyes drift closed, and she makes a soft contented sound.

I gather Keaton close to me, my fingertips stroking her bare arm. "Keat?"

"Yeah?" she says, her voice calm and happy.

"Bringing home Peaches wasn't my only surprise tonight."

She lifts her cheek from my chest and looks at me with narrowed eyes. "What else do you have up your sleeve?"

With my heart pounding out a fast rhythm, I reach into my pocket and take out the diamond ring that's been eating at me to pull out all night. Keaton's eyes widen in surprise, and she lets out a small but unmistakable gasp.

My throat has gone bone dry, but I dredge up the courage and finally say the words I've wanted to for months now. "I love you. So fucking much. Marry me, baby?"

With a quiet sob, Keaton murmurs, "Yes!" and throws her arms around my neck.

We kiss, and tears prick at the corners of my eyes. I don't think I've ever been this happy. And when I slide the ring onto Keaton's trembling finger, she lets out a sweet noise of admiration.

"You're crazy. We've only been dating for six months . . ." She can't stop smiling as she admires the way the ring looks on her hand.

I lean in and press a soft kiss to her lips. "Yeah, but we've known each other for ten years."

Her chuckle is sweet, and she places her palm against my cheek. "True. From that standpoint, I guess this was like the longest courtship ever."

"Exactly."

The crazy thing is, if someone told me ten years ago that I would eventually marry my friend Keaton, I wouldn't have been at all surprised. She's exactly the kind of girl every guy hopes to end up with—smart, hardworking, devoted, loving, and beautiful.

And now . . . she's all mine. Part of me still can't fucking believe it.

Keaton lets out a surprised squeal as I scoop her up from the couch and carry her to our bedroom, where I plan to take all night making sure she knows exactly how much I love her.

Epilogue

Keaton

"**C**HEERS," I SAY, RAISING MY GLASS OF champagne to Slate's with a satisfying clink.

His eyes hold mischief and happiness, and such a warm, comforting familiarity that it literally makes my breath catch in my chest. I haven't been this happy in . . . well, ever.

Slate leans close, pressing his lips to my neck, and all the celebratory noises in the room fade to the background. Even if we're in a bar filled with our closest friends, the only person I see is him.

"You trying to kill me with that miniskirt, babe?" he murmurs, his lips pressed to the sensitive spot below my ear. His fingers trail down to the hem of my skirt, and he grabs my ass in both hands, letting out a small growl.

I meet his gaze and give my head a shake.

"Behave, mister."

Our friend Jack was kind enough to let us rent out his entire bar for our engagement party tonight, and so far it's been perfect. The memory of dancing on this very dance floor when no one knew we were a couple yet is a secret memory I still treasure.

Sometimes I can't believe this is real life, that the nerdy girl got the hunk. But it is, and I did.

Tonight has been everything I could have ever wanted and more. Everyone is in a celebratory mood, and even some of Slate's clients—high-profile pro football and basketball players—are here to congratulate him. Newlyweds Karina and Mateo are here, and Gabby has a perma-grin every time she looks at us. Even Meera is here. It's perfect.

Slate notices my champagne glass is empty, and after a quick peck on my lips, he takes it over to the bar, refilling it and talking to Jack for a moment before returning.

"So attentive," I say, praising him as I pat his scruffy cheek. I still hadn't gotten used to the fact that I could just touch Slate freely now. That he was mine.

"Pussy-whipped is more like it," our friend Camden says, jostling Slate and playfully punching his shoulder.

That's rich coming from Camden. All night, I've

watched him sneak glances at his friend Natalie, who seems rather oblivious to his longing.

Camden, Jack, and Natalie have been best friends since high school, but I can't help but wonder if their friendship is as strictly platonic as they'd have everyone believe, or if there's something more between Camden and Nat.

But I don't wonder long, because the next thing I know, Slate is intertwining his fingers with mine and whispering in my ear. "I'm stealing you away."

Chill bumps race down my spine as his words sink in.

Giving him a curious expression, I let him take my hand and guide me to the back of the bar and down a short hallway.

Slate enters what appears to be an office and closes the door behind us. A big oak desk takes up the center of the room, with a couple of chairs and a low filing cabinet on the far wall.

But before I can get a good look around, Slate's lifting me in his arms and setting me down on the desk. Then he steps between my parted knees.

"Needed you to myself for a minute," he says at my quizzical expression. His mouth lowers to mine, and he places a sweet kiss against my lips. "Tonight's been incredible." *Kiss.* "You look amazing." *Kiss.*

I push my hands into the hair at the back of his neck and kiss him back, deeper this time, our lips parting as our tongues slide together.

A low groan rumbles in his throat. "I can't fucking wait to marry you. Can't wait to make babies with you."

"*Babies*?" I pull back a fraction. We've only been engaged a month. We've never discussed babies. Slate knows I want kids; it's one of those subjects we covered when we were friends, but I had no idea where he stood on the topic.

He meets my eyes and smiles. "I really want to knock you up. You'd look so fucking cute pregnant." He places his hand on my flat belly as he says this, and a warm shiver races through me.

I feel like someone just dropped a bomb, and now I can't get him naked fast enough. "This. Off. Now."

I'm making no sense, but Slate catches on to my rambling as I tug at his shirt. He pulls it up and off over his head, revealing his sexy, toned torso. Then he takes off my glasses and sets them on the desk beside us.

I tug at his belt, eager to wrap my hand around the erection tenting his jeans. "What did you say to Jack? I hope he doesn't think we're about to defile his office."

Slate only chuckles, his mouth moving in slow kisses along the column of my throat. "I told him I needed to make my fiancée scream my name, and he said the condoms are in the third desk drawer on the right."

"Uh, I didn't want anyone to know what we were doing in here." I groan and then swat at his shoulder.

Slate stops kissing me and meets my eyes. "Just think, after this we'll get to check *public sex* off your spreadsheet."

My lips curl up in an involuntary smile. "Hmm. I do love it when you talk spreadsheets to me."

His warm palms slide up my bare thighs. "That get you hot, baby? When I tell you we'll bang out the rest of your to-do list?"

I work at the buttons on his pants faster, and Slate only smirks.

"Gimme," I murmur, done being articulate. Although I'm a smart girl, he can make me act really stupid sometimes. And I don't mind one little bit.

"As you wish." He chuckles, drawing my panties down my thighs and helping me to step out of them.

And then we're back to kissing, and I'm stroking one hand over his thick cock, and the other along his firm ab muscles. It's too much. Too much sensation. Too much love. But then it's always like this with

Slate. He kisses and sucks and nuzzles against me, rutting his firm cock between my legs until I'm wet and aching for him.

"Condom?" he asks, his mouth inches from mine.

I shake my head, and when Slate catches the glint in my eyes, he lets out a low groan.

"Naughty girl," he murmurs, running his thumb over my sensitive core, and I shudder in his arms.

There's no one else in the world I'd rather be naughty with.

Thank you for reading about Slate and Keaton!

Continue the story in *Flirting With Forever* and find out if Camden can convince his best friend, Natalie, to be more than friends. If you liked *Love Machine*, you will LOVE *Flirting With Forever*!

Get your copy:
www.kendallryanbooks.com/books/
flirting-with-forever.

Don't Miss the Next Book

To ensure you don't miss Kendall Ryan's next book, *Flirting With Forever*, sign up and you'll get a release-day reminder.

www.kendallryanbooks.com/newsletter

Flirting With Forever

No women.

No sex.

No hooking up.

This is the oath I took in solidarity with my best friend after a particularly heinous breakup left him shattered.

No problem, right?

Wrong.

Because lately, I've begun developing big, messy feelings for our best female friend who we've both sworn was off-limits since we were sixteen years old.

I shouldn't notice the way her hair turns golden when it catches the light. I shouldn't make it a goal to see her dimples when she laughs. I shouldn't find her knowledge of current affairs so sexy.

I'm pretty sure she's oblivious, which is a good thing,

I try to convince myself. Until one night after too many cocktails when we fall into bed together. I'm left with an awkward morning-after, and one of the hardest choices I've ever had to make.

Confess how I feel, and potentially lose both of my best friends in the process, or bury my feelings and watch her move on?

How can something so wrong feel so right?

And read on for an exclusive sneak preview.

Sneak Peek of *Flirting With Forever*

CHAPTER
One

Camden

HEARTBREAK ISN'T A GOOD LOOK ON A MAN. That's an undeniable truth.

"A beer for this guy." I motion to the bartender to bring another for my miserable-looking buddy. Jack and I have been friends for well over a decade, and I've never seen him this torn up over a girl. *Ever.*

A bottle of beer appears a few moments later, and I push it closer to him. "Drink up."

"Thanks, man," Jack says, taking a long swig.

It isn't often that I volunteer to be the designated driver, but when I got the call from Jack this afternoon that his long-term girlfriend broke up with him over text, I knew he'd be drinking a bit heavier than our usual one or two reserved for Friday nights. We can't drink the way we used to in college without calling most of Saturday a complete wash.

But tonight is different. He deserves to work out his problems with his bottle of choice without worrying about getting home to our apartment safely, so I told him I'd stick to water for the evening.

"All I'm saying is she could have had the decency to say it to my face," Jack says, wiping the beer foam off his lips with the side of his hand. "What kind of person ends a year-long relationship over text message?"

"The kind of person who doesn't deserve you," I say, gesturing to the bartender for another cold one. He pops the top off a bottle for Jack and slides over a bowl of bar mix for me.

Jacksighs, sliding his empty beer bottle to the bartender. "Yeah, I guess you're right." He groans, staring down the neck of his beer like the answer to his relationship problems is stuck in there somewhere.

"Damn straight I'm right. Name one time I've been wrong in the fifteen years we've been friends."

He rests his chin on his fist but doesn't answer. Either because he can't think of a time, or because the alcohol has made his brain fuzzy.

My phone buzzes twice in my pocket—it's

Natalie, checking in to make sure I'm getting Jack good and drunk. Given the circumstances, I figured it was best that it was a "no girls allowed" kind of evening, but it's been a long time since he and I have been out without Natalie. I can't blame her for feeling a little left out.

When I glance over, I notice Jack is messing around on his phone for what has to be the tenth time tonight. The odds are good that he's already hitting up some other girl. I love Jackto death, but he's always been a bit of a player. I'm actually a little surprised his most recent relationship lasted this long.

"Natalie was checking in to make sure you were getting adequately hammered," I say, holding up my phone to snap a picture of Jack and his collection of empty bottles. He sets his phone down and poses mid-chug, giving the camera an enthusiastic thumbs-up. I send it off to Nat as evidence that I'm doing my job.

"Man, I'm so damn lucky to have you two," Jack says between long sips. "What would I do without you guys?"

A little bit of alcohol always brings out his sentimental side, but I'm game for a stroll down memory lane, so decide I'll play along.

"I hardly remember life before the three of us

were friends," I admit, shoving my phone back in my pocket. "My brain must have just erased every memory prior to sophomore-year biology class."

"The three amigos!" Jack hollers, raising his beer in a toast. "The best lab group ever!"

"Yeah, only because I carried all of our grades by doing all the work," I tease, clinking my water glass against his beer.

"Hey, it's not Natalie's fault that she was so bad at biology," he argues with a sloppy finger wag.

I guess four is the magic number of beers for Jack. I've got to remember to give him grief tomorrow about what a lightweight he's become.

"Yeah, I remember. That private school she transferred in from didn't teach bio until junior year. What was your excuse?" I pick through the bar mix and flick a peanut at Wes's head.

"Laziness, mostly," he says after batting the peanut away a little too late. It hits him square between the eyes and bounces across the floor. His reflexes are gone; he's officially drunk. "You should be thanking me. That was the class that made you want to be a doctor. I was just letting you discover your passion."

I'm a physical therapist, but same difference. "And I was just saving you from flunking science class."

Downing the rest of his beer, he shoots me the bird and reaches for the bar mix to find some ammo of his own, eventually settling on a pretzel rod. I let him take his shot, lining up the pretzel like a javelin and tossing it at me. He misses by a long shot and the pretzel goes hurtling across the bar, nailing some un-suspecting sucker in the back of the head.

"And that's our cue to close the tab." I wave over the bartender and slide my AmEx card across the bar, which gets me a confused look from Wes.

"Why the hell are you paying?" he asks, his brow furrowed. "You just got water."

"Yeah, and you just got dumped," I say, scrib-bling my signature across the receipt and stuffing a ten-dollar bill in the tip jar. "Now, come on. Let's get out of here."

As I walk and Jack stumbles across the parking lot, I shoot Natalie a quick text to let her know I've completed my mission of getting Jack drunk and that we're headed home. The radio starts as soon as I turn the key in the ignition—some catchy pop love song, which Jack immediately switches. He stays diligent on the radio dial, changing the station every time a song mentions a girl or a kiss or anything else even sort of related to romance.

I feel bad for the poor guy. Apparently, his ex has

left his heart in freaking tatters.

"All these goddamn love songs," he mumbles, throwing in the towel and shutting the radio off altogether. "I'm sick of this shit. Women suck. All they do is steal your sweatshirts and then leave when they're bored of you."

Before I can form a counterargument, he's pointing at a fast-food restaurant ahead. "Dude, let's get something to eat."

I don't even bother trying to stifle my annoyance as I pull up to the drive-through, asking the girl on the intercom to give us a minute to decide.

"What do you want, Wes? A burger? Fries?"

"I want a woman who isn't gonna completely screw me over," he grumbles, giving the glove compartment a swift kick of frustration.

"Burger and fries it is."

I place his order and pull forward to pay. Jack is either too buzzed or too sad to give me shit about paying this time, but his mood lightens a bit when I pass him the bag of hot, greasy goodness. Hopefully, those fries will soak up some of the alcohol in his system and make his hungover ass slightly more bearable tomorrow.

He tears into his fries with a satisfied grunt. "Fries are so good. Why would I need a woman when

I have fries?"

"Probably because fries can't get you off." I pull into a parking spot nearby and settle back into my seat.

"I think I've gotta go on a hiatus, dude," he says around another mouthful. "Swear off women for a while. Get my head straight."

"That's cute. But there's no way in hell you'd last more than a week. Two, tops."

As long as Jack and I have been friends, he's always had a girl in the picture. Whether it's a girlfriend, a hookup buddy, or just somebody he met on a dating app, there have been very few nights in our apartment where Jack hasn't been sharing his bed with someone. Swearing off girls will be harder for him than swearing off beer. And that's saying something.

"Bullshit. You really think I'm that weak?"

He seems genuinely insulted, so I try a gentler approach. "Come on, man. You've been getting it on the regular for as long as I can remember. There's no way you can go without."

"I've got a perfectly good hand. I'll be fine," he says into the greasy paper bag, digging out his burger. "No more women. I'm announcing it now. Hold me to it."

Resisting the urge to roll my eyes, I reach for a couple of fries. "I'll remind you of that when you meet some blonde at the gym next week and want to bring her home. You'll fold in a heartbeat."

"Like hell I will. How much do you want to bet I can make it a whole month without hooking up with anyone?"

Is he seriously going to make a wager on this? I'm not much of a gambler, but this sounds like a bet I'll be guaranteed to win, so why the hell not?

"All right, how about this." I pivot to look him straight in the eye so he knows I mean business. "I'll do it with you. No women, no sex, no hookups. I bet I can hold out way longer than you. Easy."

Jackrolls his eyes. "Oh, sure, easy for you. You're practically a monk."

It's been a long couple of months' worth of his jokes insisting that I must be a born-again virgin with how little action I've been getting. Yeah, maybe I am in the midst of a dry spell, but it's no big deal. And working long shifts in the pediatric wing of the physical therapy center certainly isn't helping.

I love my job. I really do. Not to say that I wouldn't mind getting laid in the near future. I've had a few potential prospects catch my eye, but if we're betting on it, what's another month of beating it in the shower?

"Listen, are you for real about this bet or not?"

Jack weighs it over with a few more fries, presumably trying to decide if his hand can really cut it. "You know what? Let's do it," he says, pumping his fist in the air and sending fries flying through my car.

"And whoever breaks first . . ." I chew one fry slowly, partially to build the suspense, partially to buy myself time to think of what we're betting on. A round of drinks? Cleaning the apartment for a month? No, this is some serious shit. The stakes are high. We need to make this deal worth keeping it in our pants for.

"Whoever caves first has to do the other's laundry for the rest of the year."

A sinister grin creeps across Wes's face. "Done." He wipes the fry grease from his hands onto a napkin before slapping his hand into mine.

"It's a deal then," I say with a firm handshake and a confident smirk. "So you might want to say good-bye to that hookup from last year who I've been watching you text all night. Because that's sure as hell not happening anytime soon."

My own phone chirps from the cupholder and I grab it. "It's Nat again," I say to Jack, opening the text.

Now we're all single. Lonely Hearts
Club unite.

I stare down at her message and frown. As far as I
know, Natalie is single by choice. This is the first time
I've heard her say she's lonely, and something inside
me doesn't like it.

Surely you're not lacking for
offers, Miss Moore.

She is a Moore, whether she likes it or not—a
trust-fund baby whose father's wealth is reported by
the media much more often than she would like.

Oh, hush, you can't comment on that.

Smiling, I can practically hear the sarcasm in
Natalie's text.

And why not?

Because you're a twenty-nine-
year-old doctor, for starters.
Women line up to drop their
panties for you.

I chuckle and shove another fry into my mouth.

Not interested in a gold digger.

Same. But if you know of any good
guys out there, send them my way.

A weird tingle creeps down my spine.

Will do.

"What's that look for?" Jack asks, his burger half-way to his mouth.

"Hmm? Oh, nothing." I set my phone back into the cupholder. "Just texting with Natalie."

"Good. Because now that you've taken this vow with me, Nat better be the only female you're texting with these days."

"Noted."

Why does the prospect of that not bother me in the slightest?

Acknowledgments

Thank you so much to my amazing team. Dani, Alyssa, Pam, Erin, Becca, Carrie, KP, Elaine and Flavia—you are all so wonderful and I feel blessed to work with such incredible talent. A huge thank you to my readers who make everything possible. Thank you for reading and loving my books. Every reader deserves a hot hero and a happy ending!

A big tackle hug and a butt grab to my sweet husband for supporting me in everything I do.

Follow Kendall

Follow me on BookBub to get an email whenever I release a book or have a sale!
www.bookbub.com/authors/kendall-ryan

Website
www.kendallryanbooks.com/

Facebook
www.facebook.com/kendallryanbooks

Twitter
www.twitter.com/kendallryan1

Instagram
www.instagram.com/kendallryan1

Newsletter
www.kendallryanbooks.com/newsletter/

ABOUT
the Author

A *New York Times*, *Wall Street Journal*, and *USA TODAY* bestselling author of more than two dozen titles, Kendall Ryan has sold over two million books, and her books have been translated into several languages in countries around the world. Her books have also appeared on the *New York Times* and *USA TODAY* bestseller list more than three dozen times. Kendall has been featured in publications such as *USA TODAY*, *Newsweek*, and *In Touch Magazine*. She lives in Texas with her husband and two sons.

To be notified of new releases or sales, join Kendall's private Mailing List at www.kendallryanbooks.com/newsletter.

Get even more of the inside scoop when you join Kendall's private Facebook group, Kendall's Kinky Cuties:
www.facebook.com/groups/140575819476413/

OTHER BOOKS BY
Kendall Ryan

Unravel Me

Make Me Yours

Working It

Craving Him

All or Nothing

When I Break Series

Filthy Beautiful Lies Series

The Gentleman Mentor

Sinfully Mine

Bait & Switch

Slow & Steady

The Room Mate

The Play Mate

The House Mate

The Bed Mate

For a complete list of Kendall's books, visit:
www.kendallryanbooks.com/all-books